Merrily YOURS

Editing: Sadie (Dot The i Edit)

Cover Design and Layout: Kelsey Bowman (Let's Get Lit Studio)

Formatting: Cathryn Carter (Format by CC)

Copyright © 2024 by Rachel Lewis

All rights reserved.

No part of this book may be reproduced in any form or by any electronic or mechanical means, including information storage and retrieval systems, without written permission from the author, except for the use of brief quotations in a book review.

This novel is entirely a work of fiction. The names, characters, and incidents portrayed in it are the work of the author's imagination. Any resemblance to actual persons, living or dead, events or localities is entirely coincidental.

AUTHOR'S NOTE

To my lovely readers,

I am so thrilled to return home for the holidays with the Bardot family! If you haven't read *Yours, Unexpectedly* yet, I would encourage you to do so, but this novella can be read as a stand alone. *Merrily Yours* is set about two years after the epilogue for *Yours, Unexpectedly* as the Bardot family gathers for Christmas. You'll get one chapter from each family member, giving you insight into future books while also returning to familiar characters.

Before you dive in, I wanted to include some content warnings so you are totally aware of them and can make the best choice to honor your mental health as a reader. Do what is best for you, always!

Content Warnings:

- On page explicit sexual content (see Dicktionary below)
- Swearing
- Pregnant main character (as someone who has been through infertility, it's important to me that you as the reader are aware)

Dicktionary:

- Chapter 1
- Chapter 5
- Chapter 6

xo, Rachel

PLAYLIST
Available on Spotify

If you listen to the playlist in order, there's one song per chapter and then, of course, I had to add some of my favorite Christmas songs for you as well!

1. All I Want for Christmas is You - Daniel & The Holly Jollies
2. A Christmas to Remember - Dolly Parton and Kenny Rogers
3. White Winter Hymnal - Fleet Foxes
4. Text Me Merry Christmas - Straight No Chaser, Kristen Bell
5. Last Christmas - Ariana Grande
6. A Nonsense Christmas - Sabrina Carpenter
7. What Are You Doing New Year's Eve? - The Head and The Heart
8. Hard Candy Christmas - Ralph

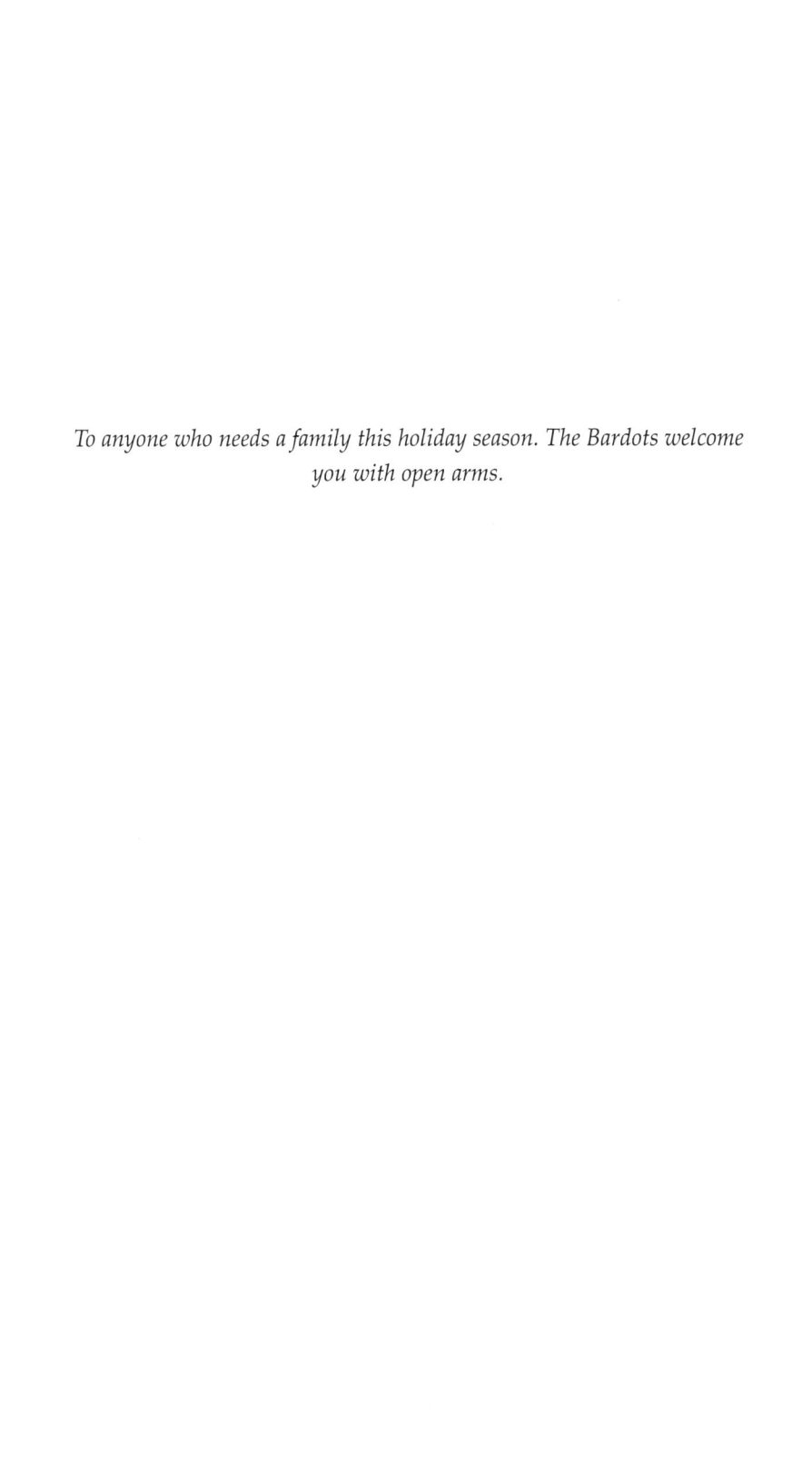

To anyone who needs a family this holiday season. The Bardots welcome you with open arms.

THE BARDOT FAMILY
~~TREE~~
Wreath

Elaine Bardot (Mom)   Hugo Bardot (Dad)

Gabe Bardot (Oldest Brother)

Jules Bardot (Twin 1)   Ben Bardot (Twin 2)

Bex Bardot-Olsson (Youngest Sister)   Anders Olsson (Bex's Husband)

Elodie Bardot-Olsson (First Grandchild)

1

REBECCA "BEX" BARDOT-OLSSON
December 19th

"There's something about a Christmas sweater that will always make me laugh." — Kristen Wiig

"Your dick is in my ass."

"Good God, Baby Bardot. You can't say shit like that before I've had coffee." Anders reaches around and rubs my protruding belly. "Also, my dick is not in your ass, but it can be. Just say the word," he mumbles, snuggling even closer.

"Okay, so it's not *in* my ass, but it is hard and you remember the second trimester horniness. I've been awake for an hour, waiting for you to put me out of my misery!"

His hand slides down my stomach and closer to exactly where I want him. He teases the hem of my panties causing my thighs to rub together searching for that delicious friction my body craves. "My poor wifey," he whispers as his fingers come further down, tracing the inside of my thigh.

I arch back into him, rubbing said ass over his morning wood, silently begging for release. I'm almost twenty-two weeks pregnant and the hormones are raging. But I'll take second trimester horniness over first trimester nausea any day.

"El still sleeping?" he asks, referring to our one year old. I nod in answer—she's an incredibly sound sleeper.

I found out I was pregnant the first time the day Anders had his Broadway debut. It was one of the best days of our life, and I still can't believe we have a daughter. She's perfect—of course she is. Except for her lack of red hair, which I constantly give Anders shit about. We weren't exactly trying for Elodie, but we weren't exactly preventing either. An unexpected joy, just like a lot of our life together.

Then, four months ago, we found out about another unexpected surprise. We really should find a better birth control option…

Anders finally gives in, breaking me out of my thoughts by running a single finger from my opening up to my clit. "Fuck, yes. Please, more." All it takes is that one touch and incoherent words are tumbling out.

"You've always been so pretty when you beg," Anders' lips whisper against the shell of my ear, and my whole body shudders. His tongue charts a path down my neck, biting where it meets my shoulder and pushing his finger into me at the same time.

I moan, grinding down onto his finger, gasping when he curls it. Unsurprisingly, Anders has spent the last four years meticulously studying my body. The thing that did surprise me, however, is that every time we are together like this it gets better and better. You hear about how your love grows the longer you are with someone—my parents are a sickening example of that—but no one talks about how the sex keeps getting better too.

Well, Mom probably has said that before, but I try to tune her out when she starts talking about the joys of sex.

Anders pulls me back to the moment with another nip to my ear. I push back into him and revel in the increasingly frantic pace his finger is setting. He pulls out and circles my clit once, twice, before reaching past me to grab our favorite toy out of the nightstand drawer—a bullet vibrator I named Buzz Lightyear. Anders had a good laugh at that.

He quickly strips his boxers off, and then does the same with my underwear. I start to turn to face him, but he stops me. "I want cuddle sex," he says, positioning me back on my side so I can be the little spoon.

"You love cuddle sex."

"I love any sex with you, baby, but yes, I do love cuddle sex. Your belly is so cute—I don't want to disturb it."

I laugh at that. "Disturb it?"

He turns the vibrator on and positions it over my clit, effectively silencing me. "Yes, disturb the baby. Or hurt them. Can I hurt them when I have sex with you? You are so strong, yet also seem so delicate when you're pregnant." He kisses my shoulder softly as if to punctuate that statement.

Shaking my head, I reply, "You won't hurt the baby. Also, can I tell you what it is—"

"Don't you dare!" He pulls the vibrator off as punishment for even suggesting that I might spoil the gender surprise for him. "You know I want to find out as my Christmas present!" he grumbles.

I am a terrible secret keeper, and this has been the hardest secret to keep since finding out the sex of the baby at our anatomy scan a week ago. I had to find out with Elodie. As a first time mom there was enough change, I couldn't also deal with the unknown of what was growing in my stomach.

This time, I wanted to find out, Anders wanted to keep it a surprise. We finally compromised, deciding that I could surprise him as his Christmas present, but I'm dying to spill!

Grabbing his hand and moving it back where I want it, I reluctantly agree to keep my lips zipped a little longer. "Okay, killer. I won't spoil it for you. Promise."

I'm rewarded with a searing kiss as Anders continues to work me closer and closer to the edge. I tilt my hips and reach behind me to position him at my entrance. It takes a little finagling, but this has been our favorite position ever since I started to really show a few weeks ago, and I know it will continue to be as the baby keeps growing.

After a moment, Anders slides in, filling me perfectly. He works in and out slowly, rhythmically, driving me to madness before slowing back down again.

"Anders!" I whine, after he does it again. "Please let me come."

"You know I can't resist when you ask so nicely," he says before picking up the pace with his thrusts and the vibrator. It takes mere seconds for me to combust, and he quickly follows into orgasmic bliss. I feel exhilarated and exhausted all at once, and I could definitely fall back asleep now. "Go pee before you fall back asleep," Anders warns, reading my mind as he tends to do.

"Marriage is so romantic," I quip.

"No UTIs on my watch," he mock salutes.

We take care of business and then cuddle back in bed. Today is a rare lazy day since we are heading back to my hometown, Sassafras, for the week. It will take a few hours to drive there, but we aren't expected until dinner, so we can doze back off until Elodie wakes up.

Which is exactly what we do.

"How many sweaters is too many sweaters?" I ask, my suitcase already overflowing.

I'm a terrible packer—always have been. I tend to wait until the last minute and then pack entirely too many things that I don't end up wearing.

Anders walks over and assesses the five sweaters I've laid out. He picks Elodie up from where she's rolling around on the ground, blowing a raspberry on her belly. The sound of her giggle heals something inside of me every time I hear it. "What do you think, El?" he asks before saying, "You can probably do without the 'Big Nick Energy' sweatshirt."

I clutch my metaphorical pearls in outrage, offended by this suggestion even though I asked for his opinion. "Excuse me! I absolutely cannot." I pause and evaluate one last time. "I'm bringing all of them," I decide, shoving them into my suitcase. "Can you zip this up? Baby girl is tired." I emphasize that by pointedly rubbing my belly.

Anders sets Elodie down and starts zipping my suitcase, but then he registers what I said and freezes mid-zip, eyeing me suspiciously. "What did you just say?" he asks.

I feign ignorance because messing with him is always fun. "What do you mean?"

"You just said 'baby girl.' Do you mean baby girl as in *you* or baby girl as in the baby in your stomach is a girl?" He narrows his eyes at me, trying to decide what game I'm playing.

"Girl… boy… who could know. Could be both? Twins run in the family, you know."

"I know for a fact there's only one baby, Bex." He walks over to me, running a finger over my jaw and then down my neck. "You're fucking with me aren't you?"

I shrug my shoulders in response, batting my eyelashes for emphasis. "Am I?"

"Brat," he whispers, reaching behind me to land a warning smack on my ass.

I let him return to packing for a few minutes while I contemplate my next move. It's also time for El to take her nap, so I grab her pudgy hands and guide her to her small bedroom. "C'mon, my cabbage," I coo, using the nickname my mom has always called me. "Let's let daddy finish packing, and we can lay down, yeah?" She doesn't seem thrilled about leaving Anders, but she does go with me and finally falls asleep after a bottle.

When I come back, Anders has given up on packing. He pats the couch, indicating that I should sit with him. I cuddle into his side, sighing as I look at the half-packed mess we've created.

"So...Can I start calling you daddy in bed?" I trace my fingers up and down his leg, ducking my head so he can't see the smile forming on my lips.

"Jesus woman," he laughs. "You really are feeling like a brat today."

I make a show of checking my wrist which absolutely does not contain a watch. "We have a few hours before El's nap is over..."

"Insatiable," he murmurs.

But thirty minutes later I feel quite sated, thank you very much.

Mom and Dad are there to greet us when we pull up to my childhood home. The outside hasn't been decorated yet—a task Dad said he was saving until the whole family was together. We make it to Sassafras fairly frequently. It's not too far of a drive from the city and, as much as I was dying to get out, I will admit I miss this crazy town.

We are making a home in New York City, but Sassafras will always feel like home. It's where Anders and I met, avoided each other, and eventually fell in love. There's a nostalgia there that will never truly go away.

Dad comes around Anders' jeep to help me out of the front seat. "I'm not that pregnant, Dad! I can get out of the car."

He just smiles down at me. Of my entire family, Dad is the most excited to welcome the new addition. He loved becoming a grandfather when Elodie was born—they are two peas in a pod. "We have to protect my grandbaby," he says and then leans in conspiratorially. "And you can tell me what it is, you know I can keep a secret."

"I heard that!" Anders yells, opening the backdoor to help El out of her carseat.

"We actually found out that it's a baby—"

"*Rebecca!*" Anders scolds. I love when he uses my full name.

"—dinosaur. Truly a miracle." I wink at Dad and then whisper, "He's really fun to mess with."

"I can see that," Dad chuckles. He turns from me then and scoops Elodie up. "How's my favorite girl?" he asks.

"I'm fine, thanks for asking," I reply, even though I know he wasn't talking to me. We've all been replaced by squishy cheeks and baby curls.

He gives Elodie another cuddle and then hands her to me. "Anders, how can I help? I'm assuming Bex packed your entire apartment?"

They assemble at the back of the car to bitch and moan about how much I pack. I walk toward Mom, who has stayed on the porch to observe from afar. "I made some cookies, mon chou," she says as a greeting, plopping a kiss on both cheeks. "Figured you'd need a pick-me-up after your drive. And I'll take this one!" She takes El out of my arms, and I have a feeling her feet won't touch the ground the rest of the week.

"Hell yes, let's go inside. They'll get everything in," I say, gesturing to Anders and Dad as they try to figure out how to get all the bags inside in one trip. I desperately want one of Mom's chocolate crinkle cookies—my favorite holiday tradition. She only makes them at Christmas time, and my mouth usually starts watering around Thanksgiving.

Mom puts her arm around me and leads me into the warm kitchen, plating two cookies for me, and pouring a glass of milk. Elodie grabs her own cookie off the counter, already learning the joys of the crinkle cookie. "How are you feeling?" Mom asks as if I don't update her daily on all things pregnancy.

"Horny," I answer.

She throws her head back in laughter, brown and silver curls falling down her back. "Good for you," she smiles. "Enjoy it. You know it will probably go away in the third trimester, but toward the end, those orgasms can be great for inducing labor."

"I already regret telling you this."

She waves me off. "Please, I know how that baby got in there. And how this one got here, too." She pinches Elodie's chubby cheeks. "You and Anders have looked at each other with sex eyes ever since you met."

Dad walks in right at that moment, kissing my mom on the top of her head. "Some thoughts are inside thoughts, dear."

"Elaine has never had an inside thought," Anders adds. "Are we upstairs?" he asks, directing the question to Mom.

"Yes, my cabbage," she winks. "You can drop any gifts in the living room, though."

Anders nods and then makes his way upstairs. After a moment, I hear his boisterous laugh. I eye my mom who is covering her mouth and avoiding eye contact.

"Mother. What am I going to find when I go upstairs?" I ask.

"Whatever could you mean, Rebecca?"

I know I learned from the best, so I narrow my eyes and start toward the staircase. When I walk into my childhood bedroom, a large poster of my husband dressed as Hercules, abs glistening, is taped to the ceiling above the queen bed.

"Bexy, I know you always wanted a poster of me on your wall, but this feels a little extreme," Anders taunts.

"Whatever, when you and the guys go look for a tree I'm going to enjoy getting myself off to your shiny abs." I smirk.

Anders groans at that, grabbing my hips and pulling me into him. "Are you going to let me fuck you in your childhood bedroom this year?" he asks.

"This bed is squeaky as fuck," I reply. He shakes his head and then plants a quick kiss on my lips. "Pick up some WD-40 when you're in town and then we can talk," I wink.

"Can we get one of those big blowup things for the yard this year?" Gabe, the oldest of the Bardot siblings, and Anders' best friend, asks, mouth full of mushroom and leek pasta.

"Swallow, Gabriel," Anders says.

"Okay, Dad," Gabe quips at the same time Ben—my middle brother and twin to my third brother, Jules—mumbles, "How many times do you think Gabe's had someone tell him that?"

"Gross, Ben! I'm eating," I reply.

Dad chimes in, cutting off any other brotherly antics. "Sure, Gabe. We can get 'one of those big blowup things.'" He air quotes. "I thought we could get out the outside decorations tomorrow, test out the lights, and then grab anything else we need when we go get the tree."

My brothers and Anders nod eagerly, all looking like little kids again. It's cute how much they enjoy this tradition that has come to be, now that we are all out of the house. Jules and Gabe are still in Sassafras, but with Ben and I living in different places we had to make adjustments to what the holidays looked like. I guess that's a part of growing up.

"Do you have any other ideas for decorations this year?" Dad asks.

The table is relatively quiet as they ponder the question. Mom leans back in her chair and makes eye contact with me. Thankfully, we have nothing to do with this particular tradition. We'll make hot chocolate—hers will be spiked—and watch the chaos unfold. But the Bardot boys take their job *very* seriously.

"I'm just going to say it," Ben starts. "I think we should do colorful lights this year." Jules and Anders groan.

"The white lights give such a classic look," Jules counters. He may look practically identical to Ben, but they couldn't be more different.

"What if…" I start, dragging my pause out for emphasis. "Well, the house is nice and symmetrical. We could divide it down the middle—team white lights could decorate one side and team colorful lights can do the other. Mom, Elodie, and I will be the judges."

Gabe leans forward. "What does the winner get?"

"That's the best part." I shrug nonchalantly and rub my belly. "The winner gets to be Santa this year."

A collective gasp echoes through the dining room. Ever since we were old enough, one of us has gotten the coveted responsibility each year of being Santa for the whole family. It means we are in control of who gets to open what presents and in what order on Christmas morning.

Everyone is extra nice to that year's Bardot Santa in hopes that they'll get to open their gifts first. It's so silly, but I know they all want it.

"But if we're in teams, there will be two winners," Anders breaks the silence.

"Obviously, rock paper scissors will determine who Santa is," I say.

Anders gasps, Gabe's eyebrows scrunch in, and Ben drums his fingers together.

"Best two out of three?" Jules asks, and I know I've got them.

"Best two out of three," I confirm.

"Deal," they reply in unison.

"You're diabolical with that Santa plan, Baby Bardot," Anders says as we snuggle into bed later that night. "You have to help me win."

"I will not!" I reply. "It's every Santa candidate for himself out there."

"I don't get an advantage for sleeping with one of the judges?" he asks. "What kind of democracy is this?"

"There are no rules at the North Pole, I'm afraid."

"Seems like the elves would riot."

I roll over to face him. "Oh, they do. Don't you remember the year they fought for elves rights and no one got presents?"

"I feel like that was just Elaine and Hugo's way of punishing you four for causing chaos."

"Could be. Dad did end up giving in and giving us our presents, so maybe this is all just lore. Who could know?"

"Who could know?" he echoes, chuckling and pulling me to lay on his chest.

We lay in silence for a few minutes before Anders says, "I'm glad to be home."

"Me too, killer. I miss it here."

"We'll move back one day," he promises. "Elodie loves it too."

I sigh. "I'd like that. I'm happy in the city, I really am…" I can feel him nod against the top of my head. "And I'm happy to support your dreams. We could stay in the city if you wanted to keep acting for the next thirty years."

"We'll just keep our options open, yeah?" he asks.

"Yeah," I agree.

I keep my head on his chest and listen as his breaths even out. I'm getting close to falling asleep when he says, "The poster is a little creepy, isn't it?"

"But in, like, a hot way," I reply. "We should take it home with us."

"How did she even get it?" Anders asks.

"I don't question Elaine's ability to get shit done. Weirder things have occurred in this house."

"True," he muses.

"Go to sleep, killer."

"I love you, Baby Bardot."

"I love you too… daddy," I tease.

"Weirdly, I didn't hate that."

He twirls a curl around his finger until we both drift off, happy to be home for the holidays.

HUGO BARDOT
December 20th

"Christmas is a box of tree ornaments that have become part of the family." — Charles M. Schulz

I left my sleeping wife in bed this morning as I slipped into my fleece lined house shoes and made my way to the kitchen. It's quiet this early, but the house feels more alive when some of the kids are staying here. I have a feeling Bex, Anders, and Ben will sleep as late as Elaine. Jules is the only one who has ever gotten up with me, but he won't spend the night here until Christmas Eve. Elodie might join me soon, but she's a pretty good sleeper, too.

I brew a large pot of coffee and grab the paper off the front porch. All Sassafras residents get their town gossip from the *Sassafras Gazette*—a paper that is as old as the town itself. I like that we still get a physical paper, so I get my town news from that and then read *The New York Times* on my iPad when I want real news.

Settling into a stool at the kitchen island, I open the paper and start reading. My phone chimes next to me, and I look at it to see a text from Julien asking if I'm awake. I'm not a big texter, so I pick up the phone and call him instead.

"Obviously, that's a yes," he answers.

I laugh at the moodiest of my four children. "Yes, Julien, I'm awake. Everything okay?"

"Yeah, I wanted to come over and have coffee there but didn't want to wake you if you were sleeping in."

"I can't remember the last time I slept in," I reply. "Come over, Son. I'll have a mug ready for you."

"Thanks, Dad. Anyone else up?"

"You know the answer to that question."

He huffs. "Yeah, I do. Okay, well I'll see you in a bit. Need me to grab anything on the way over?"

"No, I was going to make some cinnamon rolls, but we have all the ingredients. See you soon."

We hang up right as the first pot of coffee finishes brewing. I grab a mug from our collection of mismatched holiday cups and savor the rich aroma that comes with the first sip of coffee of the day. There's nothing quite like it. Bex, Jules, and I drink our coffee black—as God intended. I pull another mug down for Jules but wait to fill it until he gets here.

I'm perusing the top stories of the day in Sassafras town news when I hear a car door slam out front. Peeking out the window, I spot Jules. His hair pulled back in his signature low bun, scowl on his face. I pour his coffee and set it on the counter in front of the stool next to me.

He lets himself in and gives my shoulder a squeeze when he gets to the kitchen.

"Thanks for making coffee," he says, our mutual appreciation for the drink evident in his sincerity.

"Of course." We sit in silence, both taking the occasional sip. I read the paper and Jules spends time in his own head, a place he prefers. He doesn't talk much, but he's wise beyond his years when he does open his mouth.

"The *Sassafras Gazette* says The Coffee Shop is going to be up for sale soon."

Jules takes another sip and rolls his eyes. "I'll believe it when

I see it. There's been rumors of Ethel and Albert selling for years, and they never actually do."

I nod. "I don't know. This could be the time. Albert is getting older and that place could use a change of ownership..." I let the thought linger.

Looking at me out of the corner of his eye he says, "Are you implying something, Dad?"

"What would I be implying, Julien?" I ask.

"I don't know, maybe that I should take over The Coffee Shop?"

"Wow! That's a great idea!" I reply, really committing to the bit. "I think you would make an excellent business owner. But you are really happy in your current job, so maybe I'm way off here."

Jules is a music teacher at the high school, and I know he's been unhappy in that position for a while. He enjoys teaching private lessons to students who want to study their craft, practice, and improve. Most of the high school students are not that way, however, which has been incredibly draining. He's always talked about owning a small business—giving back to the town that has given him so much.

I think he's already doing that, but what do I know.

"The Coffee Shop does make the best coffee. Albert and Ethel should stay on, you're right."

"Woah woah woah. Coffee Shop coffee has gone downhill in the last few years, and you know it. They aren't even sourcing locally anymore, and they've been brewing their espresso at one hundred seventy-five degrees which is twenty degrees below what's recommended," he rants.

I hum, knowing I won this round. "Interesting. Seems like you know a lot for someone who isn't interested in taking over."

He pushes up from his seat and runs a hand through his hair, messing up his bun. "I'm going to wake Ben up." And with that, he walks out.

I spend the next several minutes finishing my coffee before

getting up to preheat the oven and start on the cinnamon rolls. A grumpy Jules, an even grumpier Ben, and a beaming Elodie join me in the kitchen. Ben beelines to a spot at the table, laying his head down and almost immediately dozing back off. Jules comes to the counter next to me, Elodie in his arms, and starts a one-handed attempt at spreading the filling across the rolled out dough.

"I'm fine," he says, sounding like he's trying to convince himself more than he's trying to convince me.

"I didn't say you weren't," I counter.

"If the right opportunity came along, I would consider it. I want to continue to build a life here… I—I just feel a little directionless."

"You'll figure it out, Julien. I'm proud of you for listening to your heart. The right opportunity *will* come along, and you'll be rewarded for your patience."

He nods, setting El down on the counter so he can roll the dough for me to cut. The oven dings indicating it's done preheating which causes Ben to shoot straight up. "I'm up! I'm up," he repeats.

Jules smirks. "Sit down, you shithead. Sugar and cream in your coffee?"

Ben grins back at his twin. "You know how I like it, baby."

It's good to have them home.

―――

Cinnamon rolls have been eaten, a second pot of coffee was brewed, and everyone is lazily draped across either a kitchen chair or a piece of living room furniture. Bex's head is on my shoulder, and her coffee is resting on top of her belly. I smile because I can't help myself. I'm so damn happy to have another baby running around. Elaine knows I would have had ten more, so it's probably good that she forced me to get a vasectomy all those years ago.

Being a grandparent means I get all of the perks and less of the late nights. I love when we get to have Elodie over, and I will spoil this next little dinosaur rotten, too.

I sigh and I look around, cataloging my family. Anders is on the floor stacking blocks with Elodie. Gabe wandered in shortly after the cinnamon rolls finished baking—his timing has always been impeccable—and is now helping Elaine do the dishes. Jules and Ben have opened up a puzzle and are arguing about the best way to put it together. It reminds me of when they were all teenagers.

"Think everyone will be ready to go in about an hour?" I ask. There is usually slim pickings on decor and trees this late in the season, but it doesn't feel right decorating without everyone here.

The boys all acknowledge me with nods. Bex finishes her coffee and gets up to stretch. "I think I'll go lay down for a nap," she says.

"Didn't you just get up?" Ben asks, earning a glare from Anders and a smack across the back of his head from Jules.

"She's growing a baby, dumbass," Gabe chimes in. "She can sleep whenever the fuck she wants."

"Language, my cabbage," Elaine warns, looking pointedly at Elodie.

"Seriously, Mom?" he whines. "You talk about sex all the time, and I can't say the word fuck? I'm sure El's heard worse."

"Seriously, Gabriel. My house, my rules." She smirks, and we make eye contact. We both established a long time ago that we weren't going to censor our kids, especially now that they are adults. But it's still fun to poke at them.

"Should we start a holiday swear jar?" I suggest. "Proceeds go to the Sassafras food bank?"

"I love that idea, dear!" Elaine says. "See, boys, generosity is sexy. Your future partners will thank me."

A collective groan rises. "That's my cue," Bex concludes, leaving the rest of us downstairs.

"Alright, everyone, one hour until we leave. And remember—Santa privileges are on the line. I would suggest meeting with your teammate and devising a plan," I say.

Jules comes over to sit with Anders and Elodie, immediately pulling her into his lap. Gabe finishes the dishes and joins Ben at the table. Elaine and I smile at each other across the room, eager to watch the antics unfold.

"This is the perfect tree—I mean look at it! Excellent shape, symmetrical branches! Sure, it's a little short but it's better than that monstrosity!" Gabe fires.

"Are you kidding me? That thing is like four feet tall. We can't use it as our main tree. This one is quirky, sure, but at least we can't have a conversation over the top of it," Jules argues.

"I agree with Jules, the taller tree is the clear winner," Anders chimes in.

"Et tu brute?" Gabe eyes his best friend, shock written across his face.

"Let's get both. They could look nice next to each other! Like our own little tree farm," Ben suggests.

"I like where your head is, Ben," I encourage, clapping my hands together. "Both it is."

We have already loaded the car down with all manner of outdoor decorations, from lights to blow up displays to fake reindeer, so I'm not quite sure how both of these trees are getting home, but we'll figure it out.

I pay the nice high school kid running the register, and we carry both trees to the car. The tree lot is only about a mile from our house, so the boys get to tying them down as best as possible, and then Anders and Gabe hang out either side of the back seat, arms holding them in place. When we get home, I honk several times laughing as Elaine, Bex, and Elodie scurry onto the porch.

"What in the *Christmas Vacation* is happening here?" Bex yells across the yard.

"We couldn't decide on a tree!" Anders answers his wife.

"So you bought two? Is one of them for Elodie?" She tilts her head. "It looks so small."

Simultaneously, we all look at Gabe who has his eyes narrowed at Anders. "Did you tell her to say that?" he accuses.

"When would I have been able to tell her that? I've been with you the whole time!"

"I haven't been able to trust your loyalty ever since you picked her over me," Gabe complains.

"Dude," Anders whispers. "You know you're always my number one Bardot man. But have you seen your sister's ass?"

"None of us needed to hear that," Jules replies, matter of factly.

Anders just shrugs, hopping out of the car and running to greet Bex. "How are my babies?"

"Get your head in the game, killer! If you want to be Santa, you can't let your hot wife distract you," she replies.

"You're right," he nods. "It's just…" He leans down to kiss the top of her head. "The belly really does it for me."

It's all hands on deck as we unload the new items and get other decorations down from the attic. Everything is laid out on the front lawn, making it look like a Christmas garage sale is about to take place. We haven't had a big snow yet, and the sun is shining just enough today that it's comfortable for the girls to sit and watch the chaos for a while. They make their way across the lawn and settle into three camp chairs—we bought a kid size one for Elodie—with large mugs of hot chocolate and multiple blankets to keep them warm.

Before Bex sits down, she cups her hand around her mouth and shouts, "Let the games begin!"

Anders and Jules head toward the left side of the house while Gabe and Ben focus on the right side. It takes some time, but eventually we start to see their visions come to life. I bounce back and forth between teams, naming myself Switzerland for the sake of keeping things fair.

"Dad! Can you find a plug for this blowup?" Gabe calls across the lawn. He has now blown up seven different figures ranging from a Santa that pops out of a chimney to a family of elves that flap around like those long inflatables on used car lots. The one he needs help with appears to be a Yeti. He and Ben are definitely going for quantity over quality.

On the opposite side of the yard, Anders and Jules are stringing sparkling snowflakes from the large tree. It goes surprisingly well with the large ornament garland they spent about an hour making.

Bex, ever the supportive spouse, is heckling Gabe and Ben between sips of hot chocolate. I walk over to join her after finding yet another extension cord for Gabe to use.

"Maybe cool it on the taunting," I suggest.

"Have you met Gabe? He taunts people in his sleep—he can handle a few good natured comments," she replies.

"Since when is 'Your decorations have little dick energy' a good natured comment, my cabbage?" Elaine asks, earning narrowed eyes from Bex.

She ponders her answer for a moment before relenting. "Fine, maybe that one wasn't exactly good natured." Just then a shiver wracks through her. "Alright, my hot cocoa is cold and there's no alcohol in it to warm me up, so I'm headed inside. Come on, El." She looks toward Anders. "Kick ass, killer!" she adds before packing up her things, taking Elodie's hand, and making her way into the house.

"Think we can be done in an hour, boys?" I ask. A chorus of yeses echo out, and I pull out my phone to set the timer.

———

"Five, four, three, two, and one—time!"

Anders, Jules, Gabe, and Ben all put their hands up after

spending the last five minutes frantically adding their finishing touches. It's almost dark outside and we sent Elaine into the house about thirty minutes ago so we could do a big reveal. "Bring it in," I call, watching as the boys jog toward me.

"I'm proud of you all for your hard work and dedication. Each concept was…unique"—I eye Gabe—"and well executed. Your mom and sister will have a tough decision ahead of them."

"Bex is biased," Ben coughs into his hand.

"I'll make sure the final decision is fair, don't worry. Should I go get them?"

"Wait!" Gabe says, putting his hand into the middle. "Band of Bardots on three."

Everyone else puts their hand in. "One, two, three—"

"Band of Bardots!"

"Well, that was adorable," Elaine says from the porch. "Are you ready for us?"

"Yes, dear." I wink.

While Elaine, Bex, and Elodie go back to their chairs, I take a moment to appreciate everything my boys have put together.

It's beautiful.

It also looks like Dr. Jekyll and Mr. Hyde decorated our house, and I'm sure the neighbors will have some thoughts.

Anders and Jules created a winter wonderland complete with what has to be close to a hundred snowflakes of various sizes hanging from every branch on our large elm. Their side of the roof is lined with white lights wrapped around an oversized ornament garland, which matches the one around the porch railing. They have flocked greenery lining the widows and a large wreath hanging in the center of each one. A life-size golden nutcracker stands to the left of the door with three giant red ornaments at his feet. There's a potted poinsettia on each of the three steps leading up to the porch. It's classic, elegant, and *very* Jules. It seems a little understated for Anders, but stunning nonetheless.

I look to Gabe and Ben's side of the yard, and a chuckle

escapes my lips. It is an explosion of color compared to the whites, reds, and golds of the other team. Every square inch of the yard is decorated with inflatable characters. The roof is covered in a sheet of colorful lights that alternate flashes. The leg lamp from *A Christmas Story* is centered in one window, and a cutout of the Grinch stealing a Christmas tree is centered in the other. There are three different carols playing from somewhere in the yard. It's warm and chaotic all at once.

"You both have quite the decision on your hands," I say to Elaine and Bex.

"It's really…something," Bex says, hand rubbing her belly.

"I love it." Elaine grins.

I smile and tuck her under my arms, planting a kiss on top of her head. "Of course you do, darling."

They deliberate for several minutes, walking around the yard, taking time to notice all of the small details. All four boys stand down by the street, nervously awaiting the final verdict. Elodie toddles around, laughing every time the inflatable Santa pops up from his chimney.

I watch as the girls walk back toward me. "Have you made a decision?" I ask.

"We have," Bex replies. "Though, they won't be happy about it."

"Let's go tell them," I say, faux-seriousness in my tone.

"Boys, you've done a great job!" Elaine starts. "Bex and I each scored you out of five on three different categories: originality, use of space, and creativity. The final tally was one point apart, but the winner is…"

I drum roll on my legs, for dramatic effect.

"Gabe and Ben!" Elaine shouts.

"Rebecca! I trusted you!" Anders sulks. "You, too, little gremlin," he says, picking up his daughter and bopping her on the nose. Gabe and Ben jump up, chest bumping each other.

"Killer—don't be mad," Bex pleads. "They outscored you in the originality category!"

Anders narrows his eyes. "You owe me," he murmurs before reaching out to shake Ben and Gabe's hands. "Good game, you guys."

"Love the sportsmanship!" I clap Anders on the back. "Okay you two, time for rock paper scissors. Best two out of three."

Ben and Gabe square up while Anders comes behind Gabe and rubs his shoulders. "Focus, Gabriel. You must win if I'm not in the running."

Ben turns to Jules. "What about me? Are you going to hype me up?"

"Don't fuck up," Jules says as his way of encouraging his twin.

"Wow, thanks, Jules. What would I do without you?" Ben asks.

"Probably fuck u—"

"Alright, here we go," I interrupt. "Rules are simple for rock paper scissors. Rock beats scissors, scissors beats paper, paper beats rock—"

"I never understood that one," Anders mutters to Bex who just pats him on the cheek.

"—and every one must choose their hand on 'shoot.' Cheating is automatic disqualification. First person to get two wins is this year's Santa. Here we go."

We gather around and watch the competition begin.

First round: Gabe chooses scissors, Ben chooses rock. One point for Ben.

Second round: Gabe chooses paper, Ben chooses rock. One point for Gabe.

Everyone around them leans in, ready for the tie-breaking round. You can feel the tension in the air as Gabe shakes out his shoulders, and Ben cracks his neck. They both take a deep breath and get into position.

Rock.

Paper.

Scissors.

Shoot.

Gabe chooses scissors, Ben chooses paper.

We all scream and pile on top of Gabe, rubbing his head and slapping his back. Even Ben joins in on the fun, putting Gabe in a headlock and telling him, "You better give me the first present, asshole." I think I even see a tear in Gabe's eye. Elodie is clapping wildly, though, I doubt she really understands what's going on—she's just happy that everyone else is happy.

Elaine and I hang back as all of the kids tumble up the lawn and back into the warmth. I turn to my wife of thirty years and pull her in for a kiss. She wraps her arms around my neck, and I run my hands up and down them to warm her.

"Today was fun," she murmurs, pulling away slightly.

I nod in agreement. "You raised some weird kids."

"They're pretty amazing, aren't they?"

Looking around the yard, I sigh. "Yeah. They really are."

3
JULIEN "JULES" BARDOT
December 21st

"Christmas is a time when you get homesick, even if you're home." — Carol Nelson

Music ebbs and flows through my headphones as I listen back to the recording for the umpteenth time. Something is off, but I can't quite put my finger on it. I pull my long hair out of its tie, only to retie it back in the same way.

Tapping on my legs to match the rhythm, I let the melody wash over me. The issue is tickling my brain, I just can't quite figure it out, which is annoying as fuck. It's *right* there, out of reach in my mind. I circle my fingers around my temples, close my eyes, and lean my head back to rest on the couch cushion.

A hard flick hits me right in the forehead. "What the f—"

I open my eyes and am greeted by a waterfall of curly hair that matches mine. Bex has her hands on her hips, pregnant stomach sticking out. She looks less than impressed, and I check my watch to see that it's fifteen minutes past the time she said she would be here. I pause the music and take off my headphones, allowing the sounds of life back in.

"You're late," I grumble.

"You're moody," she retorts. "And I was here on time but you didn't answer when I knocked, and you moved the spare key. It took me fifteen minutes to find the damn thing."

"Oh yeah, sorry about that." I run a hand through my hair again, trying to secure the pieces that have already fallen out. "Gabe kept coming over unannounced, I had to make it a little harder to find."

She nods her head in solidarity, knowing as well as I do that Gabe has no boundaries, and then plops down into the big armchair. She's kicked her boots off already, presumably at the front door, so she props her feet up on the coffee table and turns her big brown eyes toward me.

"Will you get me a glass of water?" she asks. "And maybe a snack? Do you have any snacks?"

I roll my eyes because she knows the answer to that. "How snacky are we talking? A couple handfuls of pretzels or do you need me to make some macaroni and cheese?"

It's silent as I walk to the kitchen of my small home and pour a glass of water. I poke my head around the wall to see why Bex hasn't responded and watch as a single tear rolls down her cheek.

"Bex? What's wrong?" I rush over, checking for injury. "Is it the baby?" Fear like I've never known takes over. I pull out my phone, ready to call 911 if necessary.

She shakes her head before choking out, "You're"—sob—"the best brother." Sob. "Did you know that?"

Relief that there isn't anything seriously wrong with her courses through me. "For fuck's sake, BB, don't do that shit to me. I thought something was wrong!"

"Nothing is wrong." She wipes under her eye. "I just love you. You're also the best uncle."

I pat her on the leg and then stand up, taking a deep breath to calm down. "Alright, enough with the sap. I'm assuming that's a yes to macaroni?"

She nods and I put a pot of water on to boil. The truth is, I love being an uncle. I can't wait to be a *dad*, if I'm being honest with myself. But after seeing the way my parents love each other—hell the way Bex and Anders love each other, too—I know it's a unique gift to find someone you want to share your life with.

"Whatcha thinking about?" Bex asks, and I realize I've been staring into the unboiling water, completely zoned out. I enjoy spending time with Bex because she doesn't mind my brand of weird.

"I guess just thinking about Elodie and how much I love that kid. And how excited I am for another little Bardot-Olsson. I'll have to come down to the city more often." I look around my small kitchen. "And maybe I need to get a cat to keep me company."

She perks up at that. "Oooh! I mean, definitely both of those things, but I want you to get a cat! We can't in the apartment and it makes me so sad. I feed all of the strays at the park."

"I'm sure the other park goers love that."

"They can fuck right off," she replies. "The cats love me and that's all that matters."

"Lovely," I mutter, adding the dried noodles to the now boiling water. "You've really become quite the New Yorker."

"I'll always be a Sassifrasian… Sassafrasite? Whatever." She pauses, gazing down at her belly. I can tell she has more to say, so I let her be. "I told Anders I'd like to end up back here one day. When he's ready to make a career pivot of sorts. Maybe Callahan will even hire him at Hawthorne—wouldn't that be full circle?"

It would be full circle, considering Callahan's class led Bex and Anders back to each other.

"You know we miss you, but is that really what you want? To come back here after you worked so hard to get out?" I ask.

She contemplates for a moment. "I was a kid and I'd never experienced anything else before. I think maybe it's not as bad as I thought it was here, you know?"

"Yeah, I do." I smile.

Bex heaves a big sigh. "Enough about me. I can tell you aren't happy either."

I stir the macaroni, debating how to respond to that. "I'm... happy..." is what I settle on, which sounds even less convincing out loud.

I can feel her eyes roll without even looking at her. "Okay, JuJu. It's okay if you aren't though."

"It's not that I'm *unhappy*..." I start. "I just feel like something is missing. I love music. I love playing with my band. I don't love teaching, though. And I feel backed into a corner, like there aren't any other options."

I think that's the first time I've voiced those thoughts out loud. They feel selfish, which is not something I'm used to being. I blend in. I'm the easy going son, hidden behind my brothers' larger than life personalities. The quiet and broody bandmate with an ear for musical composition. The brother that's always ready to comfort and provide, no matter what I'm sacrificing personally. I know Bex understands me more than anyone else, but even she doesn't quite get it. She has Anders and Elodie, and now this baby on the way.

They're building their own family, and I feel left behind.

"There are always other options, Jules," Bex murmurs. "It might not be easy, but it'll be worth it."

I raise my eyebrow at her and she replies with, "Yeah, I heard it. I don't know what this baby is doing to me, but I'm speaking in cliches."

We're quiet as I drain the pasta, mix in the cheese, and scoop her lunch into a bowl. She takes it from me and balances it on her small bump. "You shoo quif teafing," she says.

"You should chew with your mouth closed," I reply, plopping down onto the couch.

She narrows her eyes but finishes her bite and tries again. "I'm serious, Jules. You should quit teaching."

"I'm not going to quit in the middle of the school year," I say.

"That's very admirable. However, it doesn't mean you can't start making plans for what happens next."

"Right, but what happens next?" I ask, hoping she knows the answer.

"I don't know, JuJu. That's for you to decide."

I sigh, undoing my hair and retying it again. "Enough of your wisdom. Finish your food and then we need to go shopping, yes?" I ask, very ready to change the subject.

Bex groans. "Don't remind me! How I can be married to someone and not know what to get them for Christmas still boggles my mind. But he's so hard to shop for!"

"I thought you wanted to get him something to reveal the gender of the baby."

"I do, but what? A baby outfit sounds boring. I was thinking maybe a funny shirt, but I don't know where I could find that so last minute. Let's just go to the market and maybe something will inspire me." She finishes off her mac and cheese, and I take it from her to rinse off in the sink.

"I have to pee before we leave." She rolls her eyes. "I always have to pee."

"No rush, I already found my Christmas presents so I'm just going with you for moral support."

"No one likes a bragger, Julien!" she calls from down the hall.

I've learned with Bex sometimes it's best to just keep your mouth shut.

We get to the indoor market and Bex immediately spots five different items she wants for herself and nothing that would be a good gift for her husband. We meander the aisles, picking up candles to smell, admiring the work of local artists, and taste testing different teas. I find a few of the latter that I like and end up taking a business card from the owner—an older woman who has spent years perfecting her tea recipes.

I'm pocketing it when Bex comes up behind me and asks, "What are you going to do with that?"

I don't actually know so I just shrug. It's not like this woman is looking to hire an ex-music teacher to help her make tea.

We continue on, Bex half-heartedly looking for something that "inspires" her. Out of the blue she states, "You need to find a woman to take care of."

"Excuse me?" I ask, eyebrows raised. "That's not very feminist of you."

"Not that she will *need* taking care of, but you need to find someone you *want* to take care of. Someone who will want to take care of you, too," she says, bumping my shoulder and looking around as if we'll find someone right here in one of these booths.

"That is much easier said than done." I stuff my hands in my pockets to stop myself from running them through my hair—something I've realized is a nervous habit.

"True. It's not like there's a lot of eligible women running around Sassafras," she muses. "And you're too old to go pick someone up at Hawthorne now."

"I'm only thirty, Bex, it's not like I'm ancient."

"Kind of weird for a thirty-year-old to start dating someone in college though, don't you think?" she asks.

I scoff, because now I know she's fucking with me. "Hmm, I seem to remember a certain twenty-eight-year-old dating a certain college senior not that long ago."

"That was *totally* different." She winks. "Listen, I don't care where you find her but you need a person, you know? You're lonely and unhappy, which is a terrible combination for someone as broody as you are when everything is going your way. You are like a sad puppy."

"And you give the absolute worst inspirational talks," I reply.

She holds a finger up in the air. "I resent that. Oh! Look!" She uses the same finger to point to a matching baby and adult outfit on the mannequin at a booth across from us.

I smirk. "It's perfect."

"Order some extra wontons, please!" Bex says into the phone. "Yes, I'm allowed to eat those! Ugh, put Anders on."

We finished shopping, dropped everything off back at my parents' house, and now we are on the way to Gabe's for Margarita Monday, a tradition that started years ago and has become a part of our Bardot sibling culture. If any of us are together on a Monday night, we have to have margaritas and takeout.

"Babe, will you google if I can have wontons? And if I can't, order them anyway—I don't want Gabe to know he was right. I had them with El and she turned out fine." She pauses, listening. "Thank you, love you!"

"Would it be so bad to admit Gabe is right sometimes?" I ask.

Her head slowly swings toward me. "Did you hear what you just said?"

I play it back in my head and then nod. "You're right. He's the most insufferable of the four of us. It's bad enough that he gets to be Santa this year."

By the time we get to Gabe's apartment, Anders has discovered that crab wontons are safe to eat during pregnancy much to Bex's relief. Ben joins us right as the food arrives, scrolling on his phone as he walks in.

"Did you know the apartment down the hall is available for rent?" he asks without looking up.

"Are you looking to move, brother?" Gabe lifts an eyebrow. Ben has been living and working in Boston for the last several years, with no real indication of leaving.

"I've thought about it," Ben replies. He has always been a

terrible liar—or maybe it's our twin telepathy—so I can see right through his bullshit answer.

"Damn," I say. "You've more than thought about it."

He stares at me and I stare back, unblinking.

Out of my periphery I see Anders lean into Bex and whisper, "It always creeps me out when they do this."

Ben breaks first, blinking and mumbling, "Dammit." He rubs his eyes before continuing. "I really haven't 'more than thought about it.'" He air quotes. "I looked into the apartments because being here for Christmas makes me realize how much I miss you guys, okay?"

"Okay," I reply at the same time Gabe says, "Aww." Bex and Anders eye each other as Bex rubs her belly, communicating without saying a word.

"I know Boston is only an hour away, but I can't drop in on you assholes whenever I feel like it and I get…" The sentence trails off. Ben looks up at the ceiling, blinking rapidly.

"Lonely," Gabe finishes.

Ben's throat clears several times. "Yeah… yeah."

Bex circles the counter and pulls Ben in for a hug. Gabe and Anders quickly join. Ben's head pops up, eyes still watery. "Bring it in, big guy."

My steps are slow as I walk over and circle my arms around the outside of the group hug. I want my brother back in Sassafras, of course I do. He's obviously unhappy in Boston, and the weight of his unhappiness is crushing, both for him and me.

There has to be something I can do.

Has to be a way I can help fix this for him.

But I can't right now. All I can do is hug my siblings. Hold them together literally since I am unable to figuratively.

I vow right then and there to find a way to get Ben home.

Later that night I lie in bed, running through the options. I fall into a fitful sleep and dream about having a family of my own.

My own child and pregnant wife. My own family to build.

To take care of.

To love.

The morning comes entirely too soon.

4

BENOIT "BEN" BARDOT
December 22ⁿᵈ

"What I like about Christmas is that you can make people forget the past with the present." — Don Marquis

"Ben-o-it?"

"Ethel, you've known me since I was in diapers. You know that's not how you say my name," I admonish the ancient barista behind the counter.

She winks at me, the flirt, and then hands me a coffee that I know will be subpar at best. Because that's what you get at The Coffee Shop in Sassafras, Massachusetts. Subpar coffee.

"Are the rumors true?" I prod.

Ethel's hands busy themselves tidying up behind the counter. A sugar shaker tips over and I round the counter to help clean it up. She pats me lightly on the cheek and then says, "Rumors?" Like she has no idea what I'm talking about.

Narrowing my eyes, I pin her with a gaze. "Mhmm," I draw out. My fingers drum on the countertop as I evaluate what move I'll make next in our battle of… not wits, exactly. Battle of stubbornness, maybe?

I decide to play the unaffected card, shrugging my shoulders. I grab my coffee and feel as it warms my fingers through the flimsy paper cup. I turn to walk away but feel a papery hand grip mine. Our eyes meet and Ethel nods toward the supply closet.

"You know we can't keep up these trysts, Ethel. Albert is bound to find out eventually," I tease as she tugs me along behind her.

"Oh hush, you!" She closes the door and leans in conspiratorially. "The rumors…"

"What rumors, Ethel?" I ask, feigning innocence.

She looks around as though she'll find someone else in the supply closet with us. "The rumors," she continues. "They're true."

I gasp, mostly for dramatic effect, though this is actually pretty shocking. I can feel a headache forming from how hard the wheels are turning. If Ethel and Albert are really selling the shop this time…

"I just want to clarify, Ethel, my darling"—she blushes furiously at the endearment—"that you are referring to the sale of The Coffee Shop and not the rumor about Smelly Jim changing his cologne, right?"

Her eyes almost roll right out of her head. "For heaven's sake, Benoit. Yes, I'm referring to the sale of the shop."

We both stare at each other for a beat.

"Are you interested?" she asks at the same time I say, "I want it."

She taps her chin gingerly with one wrinkled finger. "Interesting…"

"Is it really, Ethel? You know how much the shop means to us."

Ethel considers me. "I don't think I can sell to an out of towner," she concludes.

I huff, running a hand through my hair. "Darling, you know I'm a Sassifrasian through and through."

A subtle nod toward the Red Sox logo on my shirt is her only reply. I narrow my eyes in return. "You're a Red Sox fan too, Ethel," I remind her.

"Yes, but I don't live in Boston unlike some people in this closet."

It's only us in the closet.

I make what might be a rash decision when I say, "I'm moving back."

Her eyebrow quirks as she crosses her arms over her chest. "Is that so?"

"It is." I'm reassuring myself as much as I am her. "I'll be back by the summer. Let me make some arrangements—promise you won't entertain other offers," I plead.

"If you make it back by summer, I promise I won't entertain other offers," she replies, her hand shaking mine with a surprisingly firm grip.

Ethel, having apparently gotten what she wanted, then turns and walks out of the supply closet and straight into *her*.

Dammit.

I make fun of Bex's obsession with Anders' hair, but what no one else knows is how her long, thick auburn hair haunts me.

Colette Russell. Or Cole, as her friends called her.

I was not her friend.

She was my high school nemesis and always one step ahead of me—it was *infuriating*.

Valedictorian by a tenth of a point.

First place at the state debate competition by a tenth of a point.

Cross country record holder by—okay that one she actually has me beat by more than a second.

Like I said, infuriating.

"Colette," I grit out and relish watching her head whip around so fast, her ponytail hits her in the face.

I'd really like to wrap that ponytail around my fist.

"Benoit," she replies, a cool mask sliding into place. "I didn't realize you were home."

"It's Christmas," I state matter-of-factly.

"You don't always come home for holidays," she replies and then flinches so subtly, I might have missed it if I hadn't spent four years studying her tells.

"Keeping tabs on me, sweets?"

"Don't call me that," she hisses. It's too easy to rile her up.

I step closer, crowding her space. "Hmm, what should I call you instead?" I ask.

Her lips part to answer and I'm mesmerized, magnetized, ready to—

"Cole?" a deep voice cuts in. We both turn toward the sound but don't move away from each other.

We stare at him for a moment before realizing where we are, as if we are both coming out of a hate-induced trance. The man waiting for her is objectively good looking. Tall. Blond. Not her type.

She clears her throat, pulling my attention back to those parted lips. "I'm on a date," she says, watching me. Calculating her next move depending on what mine will be.

I take a step away and shove my hands in my pockets. "Of course you are," I reply. "You are almost thirty, aren't you?" A reminder that I haven't forgotten about our pact.

She glares at me and then turns without another word. Her ponytail swishing as she walks to the counter with her date.

"What the fuck was that about?"

I jump, not realizing Bex and Jules have finally arrived, just in time to witness my run-in with Colette.

"Is that Cole Russell?" Jules asks. "She looks good."

His remark is casual. And deliberate. As my twin, Jules always knows the right thing to say to bait me into a reaction.

So I just hum—something that could be an agreement, but it's probably not. Probably.

"Okay, can you both stop the weird twinning? I'm ready to sit down."

I already have my coffee, but Jules and Bex have yet to order.

I find a table for the three of us while they get their drinks from Ethel.

When they sit down across from me, I know more questions are coming so I stop them by asking, "Are you even allowed to drink coffee?"

Bex groans. "Not you too! Yes, you ignorant man. I can take care of my own body, a healthy toddler, *and* the baby growing inside me, thank you very much."

I lift my hands in surrender. "Fine, fine. I just know how much coffee Mom drank when she was pregnant with you and… well…" I let the insinuation hang in the air.

"There's actually no way you remember how much coffee Mom drank. We were two." Jules—the ever present logical mind.

"Way to ruin my fun, JuJu!" I say. "You're right, I don't remember. And you can have whatever you want," I say to Bex, leaning back in my chair. "Have a glass of wine if it'll help you unwind. Whatever you need, we can get it for you."

Bex inhales, watching to see if I'm joking or not and then quickly picks up a napkin to dab under her eyes. "For fuck's sake, why are you being nice to me?"

"Because you're my sister and I love you and I love my niece and my unborn niece or nephew. As much as we tried to make your life miserable growing up, I feel like I need to atone for some of that now," I reply.

"*We*…" Jules mutters and then he sets his hand in the middle of the table, and Bex looks at him knowingly before setting her own down on top of it. Then they both turn their gazes toward me and wait.

"Oh! Uh—is this like a little league situation?" I ask, placing my hand on top. They both nod and then pile their other hands in, waiting for me to place mine last. Bex lays her head down on her forearm and mumbles incoherently.

Jules and I exchange a look before he asks, "What was that, BB?"

She lifts her head back up, crying again. "I just really want a cold cut sandwich," she wails.

Jules nods as if he understands what that means. Trying to be helpful, I ask, "Do you... do you want me to go grab you one?" I look at my phone and see that it's just past 9:00 A.M. "I'm not sure if the deli is open yet, but—"

"I can't fucking have one," Bex cuts me off. "Coffee, fine. Wontons, fine. Cold cuts? Nope. Soft cheese? Unacceptable." She scowls down at her stomach. "I wanted cheese so bad when I was pregnant with Elodie. She was almost named Brie."

Jules and I suppress smiles. "It's not funny!" Bex exclaims, pulling her hands out of our pile.

"You're right, it's—" Red hair catches my attention. That damn ponytail bouncing up and down as Colette listens intently to whatever her moron date is saying. They find a table and he pulls her chair out, waiting for her to sit down before pushing her in, like a child. She doesn't need his help, she's a grown woman. She's probably incredibly irritated that he's still standing there as she awkwardly scratches the chair legs across the floor.

A throat clears and I realize I've been caught.

"Oh my God, you're obsessed with her." Bex's eyes gleam, like I've told her she actually *is* allowed to have a cold cut sandwich.

"I hate her." I don't hate her.

"You don't hate her," Jules says, reading my mind.

My eyes narrow. "Stop reading my mind."

"Stop wearing your mind on your face."

"That doesn't even make sense," I scoff.

"Will both of you please shut up?" Bex hisses before turning her now scrutinizing gaze on me. "So... what are you going to do about it?"

Now I'm confused. "About what?"

Bex's sigh is longsuffering. "About the fact that you're in love with her and she's on a date with another man." She throws the phrase out as if it means nothing.

In love.

Ridiculous.

"There's a fine line between love and hate," Jules interjects.

"So they say." Bex sips her coffee, considering me for a moment before coming to a decision. She opens her mouth, closes it. Does it again. And then finally shrugs her shoulders and leans back in the chair, seemingly giving up on her task.

"Giving up so quickly, Rebecca?" I ask.

"Listen, I'm too pregnant for this," she replies, rubbing circles on her stomach. "I would love for one of you to give me a sister, but I stopped holding my breath waiting for that a long time ago."

"You don't need a sister, you have three brothers!" I reply.

"Do you hear yourself?" she asks. "That's exactly why I want a sister!"

I wave her off, my attention returning to Colette and her date. She's fiddling with the rim of the coffee cup—another one of her tells that her date is completely oblivious to.

I bet he's a banker, he looks like a douchey finance bro.

"You're a douchey finance bro, too," Bex says.

I didn't realize I'd said that out loud.

"Yeah, but I'm not like *that*." I wave toward them, catching Colette's attention. She glowers at me before returning to her conversation. "He can't even properly hold her attention!"

Jules huffs. "You're sulking. Go do something about it if it bothers you that much."

I sink into my chair, thinking about what Jules is saying. Am I sulking? Do I actually care what Colette Russell thinks of me?

No.

Maybe.

Bleh, I don't like this much introspection. "So, what's new with you, Julesy?"

"Smooth transition," Bex mutters.

I ignore her.

"Nothing really. Things are good," Jules says, taking pity on me. "I did hear rumors about The Coffee Shop going up for sale. I need to ask Ethel about it." He drums his fingers on the table nervously.

I know the shop means as much to him as it does to me. He can't afford it on his teacher salary though, which is why I wanted to corner Ethel this morning. I *can* afford it on my douchey finance bro salary.

Leaning in, I whisper, "The rumors are true."

Jules' head shoots up, his eyes meeting mine. They're full of poorly concealed hope.

"Fuck," he mumbles. "How do you know?"

I shrug. "I got Ethel to admit it before you got here."

"Is that why you were in the supply closet together?" Bex asks.

"Don't tell Albert."

She mimes zipping her lips.

"How much do you think they want for it?" Jules asks.

"Doesn't matter. She said she won't entertain other offers as long as I'm back by the summer."

"You're really moving back?" Bex's shocked tone matches my twin's shocked expression.

Boston has been fun. It's got so much more to offer than Sassafras, but it's not *home*. As much as Bex teases, I am ready to settle down. Find someone who will tolerate me for more than a night. And I miss my family. After growing up attached at the hip to my siblings, I was ready to be on my own. Where I wasn't one of the Bardots, I was just Ben.

In doing that, though, I lost part of my identity.

Nodding in answer to Bex's question, I let the idea of moving back really, truly sink in.

And it feels really damn good.

Forty five minutes later, Colette is still making eyes at me as she half-pays attention to blondie. Not the good kind of eyes, however. More like she's one second away from switching seats so she doesn't have to keep looking at me.

"Okay, I'm sick of sitting here watching you drool. I'm going home to my own redhead—see you suckers later," Bex announces, sliding out from her seat and standing to leave.

"I'll head out too," Jules adds. He slides his black leather jacket on and readjusts his man bun.

I hop up too because I'm not going to stay here by myself. "I'll see you back at the house, I'm just going to say goodbye to Ethel real quick."

Bex and Jules walk away as I gather my empty cup and wave to Ethel. "Remember our deal," I call out across the room.

Colette's head whips toward me, and I relish the fact that she thought I was talking to her. I adopt a smug expression and walk toward her table, much to her chagrin.

I ignore blondie and lean down into Colette's space. "I wasn't talking about you, sweets, but I'm glad to see I'm top of mind."

She glares at me, opening her mouth before being interrupted by Finance Bro Ken. "Uh, can we help you with something?"

I keep my eyes on Colette. "I don't know… Colette, can he help us with something?"

"That's not really what I…"

"What is wrong with you?" she hisses.

I reach out and stop her hands from fiddling with the rim of her mug. "I'm just sick of watching you practically falling asleep over here. You need to be stimulated, Cole." I lean in even closer. "He's not very stimulating is he?" I whisper.

"What the fuck? I can hear you."

"And how would you know what I need?" Colette asks. "You might have known me in high school, but you don't know me anymore, Benoit." She smirks, thinking she has the upper hand.

"Oh but I do. And you hate that don't you?"

"I hate *you*," she seethes.

Somewhere in the background, I hear blondie pushing his chair back. "Woah, maybe I should…"

That catches Colette's attention. "No! Brody, don't leave. Benoit is the one who is going to leave!"

I pull up a chair instead, turning it so I can rest my elbows on the chair back and prop my chin in my hands. "Nah, I think I'll stay." I grin.

"Yeah, I'm out of here," Brody says.

"Bye, Ken!" I wave, still looking at Colette.

"Wait, Brody!" Colette gets up to follow him and then thinks better of it, instead turning her wrath on me.

"Get fucked, Bardot."

"I'm trying, Red."

She scoffs. "As if. I would never touch you with a ten foot pole."

I pointedly look over to where she's stabbing me in the shoulder with her finger. She immediately pulls back as though she's been burned.

And maybe she has.

"You're an asshole."

"And you are too good for that dickhead."

"Complimenting me now, Benoit? You've lost your touch," she snips.

Humming, I push to stand. I stare at her before doing something astronomically stupid. I take a piece of her ponytail between my fingers, wrapping it once and tugging just slightly. "Hmm…" I watch as her eyes darken. "I don't think I have."

Forcing myself to let go, I walk away.

I get all the way to the door before saying, "Seven months and two days, Colette."

I look back over my shoulder and enjoy watching that pretty mouth pop into a perfect "O."

It's good to be home.

5

GABRIEL "GABE" BARDOT
December 23rd

"Christmas is awesome. First of all, you get to spend time with people you love. Secondly, you can get drunk and no one can say anything."
— Michael Scott, The Office

"Louie's tonight?" Anders asks.

"Uno!"

Dammit, how is Bex so good at UNO?!

"Sure, I'd be down for a night at Louie's. It'll be just like old times!" I place a green two card down on the pile. We circle around to Jules who places a Draw Four card down right before it's Bex's turn again, quickly turning her expression of glee into one of frustration.

"What the fuck, JuJu!" Bex yells, startling a sleeping Elodie who passed out on the couch halfway through *The Grinch*.

"Easy there, killer," Anders soothes, massaging her shoulders. I watch as Bex leans back onto him from her spot on the floor.

"That's your name," she reminds him. And then a whimpered, "I was so close to this game being over."

"You didn't have to play with us," Ben states, handing her four new cards.

But we all know she didn't really have a choice. Sibling UNO is a tradition.

Bex remains grumpy as we continue to play. Anders tries to calm her down—it's a futile effort. I watch as he leans down and whispers something in her ear. It's been six years since they first got together, but they are still sickeningly in love.

It is hard to be around them sometimes. Between my parents, and my best friend and sister, all I see is perfect relationships around me. A reminder that I've fucked up every relationship I've ever attempted. Not that I've tried that hard since—

"Uno!" It's Ben this time.

"Well, shit," I mutter as I draw another card.

We play until it gets back to Ben, all of us watching as he lays down his last card. He hops up and does a bizarre victory dance that looks like his rendition of the macarena.

"After that display of athleticism, I feel like you all need some hot chocolate!" Mom pops her head in from the kitchen. Everyone nods enthusiastically and she disappears around the corner again.

"So, we are good for Louie's tonight? Maybe after dinner?" I ask.

"I'll drive," Anders winks.

Mom walks back in with a tray of hot chocolate. She hands a mug to Bex first who asks, "Mom, can you watch El tonight? I think we're all going to go to Louie's after we put her to bed."

"Of course I'll watch my favorite baby!" Mom exclaims.

"We were all replaced the second that pregnancy test was positive," I sigh.

Anders hums. "She's definitely way cuter than all of you. She gets that from her mother"—he leans down and kisses Bex's cheek—"and her grandmother," he finishes, winking at Mom.

Ben, Jules, and I groan. Anders is such a suck up.

We continue talking and drinking our hot chocolate before parting ways to get ready for dinner.

It's been really nice to have everyone in town for the holidays. We don't get the same hang out time we did growing up. We fought like crazy, sure, but when you have three younger siblings that are so close in age—it's a bond I've taken for granted in the past.

I head up to my old childhood bedroom and flop down on the bed. I live above Louie's so I'll stay there tonight, but I'm not that far from Mom and Dad's, and it's nice to be able to crash here when family is in town.

My phone dings and I pick it up to see a Tinder notification. I already know I'm not interested, however, curiosity gets the better of me. I open the app and see that I've matched with someone named Carly. I swipe through her pictures, chiding myself for how unaffected I am. She's cute, sure. She is probably lovely to be around, but her hair is black and curly when I really want it to be blonde and wavy. Her eyes a deep brown, when I prefer to drown in a sea of blue. She's tall and curvy, and yet, I find myself wishing she was petite and athletic.

Fuck.

Frustrated, I close out of the app and allow myself to drift into a fitful nap.

Louie's is full tonight. I was informed that they are hosting a Christmas Eve Eve party, which I didn't know was a thing.

We all left the house together about an hour ago and are now occupying a corner booth. Louie has decided he wants to start making specialty cocktails so we have three sitting in the middle of the table, everyone afraid to touch them. Instead, my brothers and I all have a beer, Anders has a coke, and Bex is sipping a Shirley Temple with extra cherries.

"C'mon, one of you has to try one!" Bex encourages. "I would but..." She rubs her belly and shrugs.

I look over and see Ben and Jules touching their noses—that

fucking twin telepathy at work again. "Nose goes," Ben says, eyeing me.

Fine, I'll bite.

"Which one should I try first? The homemade Wassail, Christmas punch, or Santa's Snowball?" I ponder.

Jules grimaces. "What the fuck is Santa's Snowball?"

"Louie said something about Amaretto and ice cream? Maybe brandy? He rattled off so many ingredients, I stopped paying attention," Anders admits.

"I'll try that one first…" I take a sip, acting as though I'm at a wine tasting. The liquid swirls in the glass before meeting my tongue and *damn*—that's phenomenal.

"Holy shit, that's good! It just tastes like vanilla ice cream," I say.

Bex's eyebrows lift. "Dangerous."

She's not wrong.

Another hour later and I've finished all three of Louie's specialty cocktails with the help of Ben and Jules, once they realized I wasn't fucking with them about how good they were.

"Let's get more!" Ben says as he downs the dregs of the Christmas punch. Bex and I are each sitting on the outside of the booth, so we slide out and head toward the bar to get another round.

"So, I think we've talked Ben into coming home… What about you and Anders?" I ask. I'm definitely feeling tipsy but not completely smashed. I'm on my way there, though.

Bex shrugs her shoulders, looking away. "We're not quite done in—" Her eyes widen incrementally as she rapidly looks back and forth between me and the entrance. "I swear I had no idea, I'm so sorry," she leans in and frantically whispers.

"What are you—"

"Luce!" Bex exclaims, and my ears start ringing. "I didn't know you were in town tonight!"

Luci. Fuck.

Last I checked she was teaching yoga at a wellness center in Hawaii.

Bex opens her arms, welcoming in one of her best friends. They sway back and forth a few times before Luci pulls back and looks at my sister with eyes full of love. I face toward the bar because I can only take so much torture, seeing her again.

I overhear Luci say, "Oh my goodness, look at that belly! I can't believe I'm going to be an auntie again!"

"I've missed you, Luce. El will be so excited to see you," Bex adds.

"I'm excited to see her," Luci states. "And the rest of your crazy crew."

Taking that as my cue, I inhale deeply before turning to face my biggest regret.

"Hey, Luce, it's good to see you." I dip my chin in acknowledgement.

"Likewise, Gabriel." Her skin is tan, even in December, and her blue eyes are shining. Her golden blonde hair is streaked with lighter highlights. She's definitely been somewhere sunny, then. But why is she here?

"What's with the surprise appearance?" I ask and immediately hear how annoyed I sound, though that's not my intention.

Luci flinches slightly, answering, "Oh, you know I can't commit to anything." A jab at me. "Made the decision last minute to head back here. Rosie is at Hawthorne now, so I figured we could spend the holidays together."

"You're welcome to spend them with us!" Bex says, giving me "get over it" eyes.

"No, no that's okay! I'll stop by and say hi to Elaine and Hugo tomorrow, but Rosie and I have Christmas day plans."

Louie brings our drinks, notices Luci, and comes around the bar to give her a big bear hug. "When you're done catching up with Louie, you should come sit with us."

Everyone stares at me, as though I just suggested nuclear

warfare. Luci recovers the quickest, because of course she does, and says, "Yeah, I'll meet you guys over there."

Bex takes two of the drinks and hurries back over to the booth. "Scooch together and don't be weird, Luci is here. Act normal, dammit!"

"Luci is here? I love her!" Ben yells loud enough that Luci hears him and turns around to blow him a kiss.

My insides heat, a fierce jealousy exploding throughout my body. "Don't fucking think about it," I warn, low and ominous.

Ben puts his hands up in surrender. "Damn, dude. You know I wouldn't. I'll be on my best behavior." He crosses his heart.

"Quit acting like a caveman asshole that has any claim over her, Gabriel. You had your chance," Bex seethes.

Anders rubs Bex's shoulders and she relaxes back into him. "Alright, everyone, let's calm down. We are excited to see Luci, Bex's best friend and a genuinely good human. Everyone will be normal, no one will flirt—except maybe Gabe—and we will all enjoy watching Ben continue to get smashed on Santa's Snowballs. Got it?"

"Got it," we all say, with Bex chiming in, "Yes, sir."

Ben, Jules, and I grimace at that. Anders plants a kiss on Bex's cheek.

I can't help but watch as Luci saunters over from the bar. She's gorgeous—she always has been. Her toned legs move under her jeans, strong and powerful. I've imagined those thighs wrapped around my face more than I'd like to admit. It's been fodder for the spank bank for years.

As she approaches, everyone starts to scoot around the booth, leaving a space right next to me. I slide over, accepting the inevitable. Luci plops down next to me, the thigh I was just admiring pressed firmly against mine.

"Hello, brothers Bardot!" Luci exclaims, tipping her cocktail toward Ben and Jules. "And the honorary Bardot." She winks at Anders.

"I see Louie talked you into one of tonight's specialty cocktails." Ben grins.

Luci takes a demure sip of her drink. "Yes, the Christmas punch. Not bad, actually, but very strong."

"And you're a lightweight," Bex adds. "Remember that night sophomore year—"

Luci's groan cuts through any reminiscing. "Oh my God! Don't remind me! I had three drinks, but I swear Riz's ratio of vodka to cranberry juice was ninety-nine percent vodka and one percent juice."

"We woke up the next morning on a bench in the quad," Bex giggles.

"Seems safe," Jules admonishes.

"We're here, aren't we?" Luci asks, her tone teasing. "Anyway, lesson learned! Don't let me have more than two of these bad boys tonight, got it?" She points to her Christmas punch which is already halfway gone.

Bex shrugs, eyeing me. "I don't think I'll be out too late tonight, so you're someone else's problem."

We spend the next bit of time laughing and drinking, getting progressively louder as the night goes on. Around ten o'clock, Louie announces holiday karaoke will be starting soon, and I get half-hard at the excited wiggle Luci does next to me. She's mostly through her second glass of Christmas punch, demanding that she and Bex perform "Baby, It's Cold Outside," but not the "old patriarchal one, the new one where the woman has a choice"—their exact words.

I watch their performance and try not to take in the way Luci's body moves on stage. Her voice is not half bad and acts as a siren song. I'm mesmerized by her delicate hand holding the mic, her golden waves swishing side to side, and the way her nose scrunches up when she misses a word.

"You're staring," Ben murmurs next to me, but I'm too drunk, or maybe just too distracted by her, to care.

They finish and Anders gets up on stage next to sing "Santa Baby" at Bex's request.

I'm sick of their cuteness and need a minute away from the berry scent of Luci's perfume. "I'm getting another," I say, not looking back to see if anyone else wants something. I know I'm being an asshole, but I feel so antsy, like I need to unzip myself and crawl out of my own skin.

It only takes a moment before I feel her presence behind me. "Hey," she whispers. She sits on the barstool next to me, turning so her knees brush my leg. It could be accidental, but when I look into her eyes, I realize it's not. "Sorry if I'm making things awkward." She dips her head, that confident girl disappearing before my eyes.

"Hey," I whisper back, using my hand to tip her chin back up. "Don't do that. You know you're welcome with us anytime."

She nods and leans a little more into me before I bring my hand back down to my side, willing myself to stop touching her. "It's just that Bex is like family, you know?"

I huff a laugh. "Yeah, I do know."

"Not like that." She flicks my arm. "Listen, we were both kids, okay? It's been years. I think we can move past all of"—she gestures around vaguely—"*this*."

I swallow hard. Can I move past the mistakes I made so many years ago? I really want to. So I nod. "Yeah, you're right."

She sticks her hand out for a— "You want to shake on it?" I laugh.

She nods emphatically. "Yeah… I do."

So we shake hands. And then our fingers twine together. And we don't let go.

At least, not until I catch movement out of the corner of my eye and see everyone from our table walking toward us. I pull my hand out of Luci's and miss the touch instantly. I look into her eyes expecting to see hurt, but I only see understanding.

Luci has always understood me. Even when she didn't want to.

"We're headed out!" Bex says, once she reaches us. "But you guys feel free to stay and… do whatever…"

"Subtle, Baby Bardot," Anders jokes. "Let's get home."

We say our goodbyes and then Luci turns to me.

"I guess that's our cue," I say at the same time Luci says, "I think we should go upstairs."

"You think we should…" Wait, *what*?

"C'mon, Gabe." She runs a finger up and down my arm, my skin erupting in goosebumps. "I don't think I'm misinterpreting here, am I? I'm leaving town after the holidays. We don't have to, but I'd like to spend some more time with you…"

"Mmhmm. Yeah, that. We should definitely do that." A smile lights up her face, and I'm already incredibly hard just thinking about more time with her.

I close out our tab, and Luci immediately laces our fingers together, dragging me behind her as we exit the building and walk around to the apartment entrances. I think I might be dreaming because she keeps shooting coy looks over her shoulder. We open the door and make it halfway up the stairs before my impatience and impulsivity gets the better of me.

"Wait," I say, stopping so abruptly, Luci crashes back into me.

Her hands are on my chest as she looks down through thick eyelashes. "What, Gabriel?"

"How much have you had to drink?" I ask. I had several of Louie's drinks but also had a big dinner and some snacks so I'm only feeling slightly buzzed. I watched Luci only drink two glasses of Christmas punch, but I want to—no I *have* to—make sure she consents to this.

"You saw how much I drank tonight. That's all I've had. I am a little tipsy, but we can make some coffee upstairs if that'll make you feel better."

"And you consent to this?" I ask.

She nods, licking her lips as her gaze drops down to my mouth.

Fuck. "Words, Luce. Can I kiss you?"

"Please."

"Can I fuck you?"

"Please," she whines.

"Will you stay the night?" That catches her off guard.

"Uh… maybe. I'm not—I don't know if…"

I silence her with a kiss. And it's the best kiss I've had since… Well, since the last time I kissed *her*. My hands tangle in her waves, and I give a slight tug, reveling in the gasp she lets out. My tongue reaches out and meets hers, and I can feel when she gives up and sinks into me.

"We'll talk more about that later," I concede. I don't want to ruin my chance again.

She's been acting confident all night, that's Luci's modus operandi. Fake it until you make it. But I don't want her to fake anything with me.

I take the lead now, moving around Luci and guiding us both to my apartment, the same one I've lived in since Anders and I were at Hawthorne. I keep it fairly tidy but it's definitely a bachelor pad, so when I walk in, I instruct Luci to sit on the couch, and I get a pot of coffee brewing while I clean up as much as I can.

"You don't have to pick up for me!" Luci calls from where she's gotten cozy on the sofa.

I shove some dirty clothes in the hamper before answering, "I'm not."

Her muttered, "Liar," greets me as I get two mugs out of the cabinet and pour coffee in. "Sugar?" I ask.

"Two scoops and a splash of milk, please!"

We drink our coffee and I put on a Christmas movie for some background noise. There's not much talking, but our mugs are eventually empty and our hands start wandering—familiarizing ourselves with each other's bodies.

We kissed all those years ago, but we never slept together. I can't deny how much I want it now, though.

Luci grabs my cock over the top of my jeans, and I almost come in my pants.

"Fuck, Luce. I want to last."

She giggles at that but removes her hand, moving it to safer territory.

"Bedroom or couch?" she asks.

"Bedroom," I murmur, making no move to get up. Instead, I've discovered my love of Luci's collarbones. I pull her onto my lap and kiss and suck her clavicle. I move to the base of her neck and suck *hard*.

"Gabe!" Luci scolds, but the way she grinds down on me tells me she doesn't mind. "I thought we were going to the bedroom." Her voice is light, unfocused.

Without breaking contact with her skin, I stand up and wrap her legs around my waist, carrying her to the bedroom. When we get there, I'm still not ready to break contact, so we fall on the bed together, our movements becoming frantic.

Reluctantly, I pry myself off of her and stand. She's beautiful laid out in my bed, however, we are both entirely too clothed. I reach for her pants button and undo it, pulling the zipper down slowly.

It's like unwrapping my first Christmas present, except it's Luci which makes it a thousand times better. I slide her jeans off, revealing a pair of cotton underwear that say "Monday" on them.

"It's Wednesday," I laugh.

She looks down and sees what I'm talking about. "Oh yeah, I can never find the right pair for whatever day it is. And it's not like people normally see them so…"

She lets the implication linger. I'm the only one getting to see her like this right now. And damn, I like that. I don't say anything else, instead taking the underwear all the way off and admiring her perfect body.

"You're staring," Luci says.

"Yeah, I tend to do that with you," I reply. "I can't help it. Can I?" I dip my head down and kiss her inner thigh.

"I'd like that." Luci's reply is enthusiastic. So I get to work.

One taste is all it takes for me to know that I'll be ruined for anyone else. She tastes amazing—so sweet, just like the rest of her. I find her clit and tease, enjoying the way she squirms to keep me right where she wants me.

"Luce, you are…" I lose my words mid-sentence.

"God, it's so good," she murmurs. "We shouldn't be…"

I pull away. "Should I stop?" I don't want her to regret this.

I don't want her to regret *me*.

"Luci, babe, I'll stop. Just say the word."

She whines, gripping my hair and pulling me back into her perfect cunt. "I don't want you to stop."

So I don't. I keep working my tongue, adding in a finger, and then two, until she's clenching around me and her back is arching off the bed, putting her perfect tits up into the air. I haven't even seen them yet, and I know I'm going to love them.

Luci rides my fingers and face, letting the waves of her orgasm crash over her. And I revel in every single second of it.

Luci's like a gust of wind—there one second, gone the next. I vow to enjoy every second I have with her tonight.

She comes down from her orgasmic high, mouthing, "Holy shit," as she flops onto her side. I move to crawl up next to her and she holds up a finger. "Give me a minute," she giggles.

"Yes, ma'am." That earns me another laugh.

I stare at her, engrossed in the way her chest rises and falls. Before I can think twice about it, I get back on my knees and slowly pry hers open. I'm fucking hard and I want another taste of her, if she'll let me.

"I don't think I can…" she starts when I drag my finger through her slick.

"Let me try?" I ask.

She nods her head. "O-Okay."

I start slow, playing with her as I watch her face for her reaction. She's tight around my finger, so I add another one, stretching her. I curl my fingers forward, and she lets out a delicious moan. I'm so turned on. She's gorgeous and I want more.

I bend to lick her opening, but she abruptly sits up and strips her top off.

I was right, I love her tits.

"Bra, too," I rasp.

She complies and I'm greeted by pert, rosy nipples. "Fuck."

Luci lays back down. "Yeah… do that."

Resuming my previous activities, I lick and suck Luci's clit, working both of us higher and higher. I'm trying so hard to last for her, but I don't know if I can.

Luci reaches up, pinching her nipple between two fingers. One twist, two—

And I'm coming in my pants.

Fuck she's hot. She's coming too, and I'm now obsessed with the look on her face when she loses control.

She's always been a free spirit, but I've understood from the beginning that it's a mask.

I understand because I do the same thing.

Luci props herself on her elbows, her chest rising and falling rapidly. "I've never done that before."

"You've never…"

She must see the look of horror on my face because she quickly amends, "No, no! I've done that! But no one has ever made me come twice by going down on me." She smirks. "Should I return the favor?"

Oh shit. "Well, I… uhm. I kind of already…" I can feel my face getting red, adding to the embarrassment of this moment.

"You… Oh!" Her eyes widen as she looks down at my stained pants. "Just from eating me out?" The astonished look on her face makes me smile.

"Yeah, Luce. Just from eating you out."

"Also a first for me," she replies.

We clean up and I get her a T-shirt out of my drawer. I like seeing her in my shirt. I don't ask, I just pull her in to be the little spoon before drifting off into the most restful night of sleep I've had in a long time.

Content. This must be what it feels like to be content.

———

The sun slices through my gauzy curtains, slowly urging me to wake up. I stretch, reaching for the beautiful woman who has occupied my mind for years.

Only, she's not there.

The sheets are cold and my T-shirt has been folded neatly, laid flat on top of the dresser. There's a Post-it on my nightstand.

"'Thanks for a good time. Merry Christmas. Xo, Luci.' What the fuck?" I crumple it up and throw it across the room.

I should have guessed, but I thought she'd stay. I really thought she'd stay.

I drag myself out of bed, walking across the room to pick up the little piece of her that she left behind. I smooth out the Post-it and put it on top of the shirt I'll never be able to wear again.

Merry fucking Christmas to me.

6
ANDERS OLSSON
December 24th

"Let's be naughty and save Santa the trip." — Gary Allen

Damn.

My wife is hot.

Seeing her pregnant is definitely addicting. I loved it the first time around with Elodie, and I love it even more now that I can watch her blossom in motherhood. She continuously amazes me. Growing a human inside you? I can't imagine. Growing a human inside you while keeping up with the toddler terror? The woman deserves a medal.

Or an orgasm.

We are going ice skating with the family today, so the orgasm will have to wait. I would be lying if I said I hadn't thought about taking my wife in her childhood bedroom though.

Focus, Anders. We have a little human that needs to get out the door.

I chase Elodie around with her snowsuit, which I realized was a mistake as soon as she started giggling. She's decided we are playing a game of keep away from Daddy that has now turned into keep away from any adults. El was an early walker which has turned into a speed demon toddler.

"Elodie Elaine Bardot-Olsson! Get back here or we can't go ice skating!" I call after her.

"Damn, that's such a mouthful," Gabe chimes in, rather unhelpfully.

"Language, Gabriel," Bex scolds from the couch where she's struggling to get her snow boots on.

"Damn! Skate-ing!" Elodie screeches from down the hall. Bex shoots daggers at Gabe who is trying desperately not to laugh.

I ignore them both and round the corner into the kitchen where I find Elodie sitting calmly on the counter. Elaine is next to her with a plate of powdered sugar donuts and a glass of chocolate milk. My mother-in-law gives me a look that seems to say *Try me*, so I just raise my hands in surrender and approach the scene slowly.

Elodie, now distracted by sugar, lets me put her pudgy little arms and legs into the snowsuit before zipping it up. "Doh-doh, Dada!" Elodie holds a donut up to my face, and I pretend to take a bite.

"Yummy, El! Delicious donut!"

"De-lis-is!" Elodie repeats. Bex waddles in holding tiny snow boots and thick socks. El wiggles her toes and giggles at her mom, her chocolate curls bouncing as she belly laughs.

"Anders! Distract her, please," Bex requests.

I twist one of Bex's curls around my finger and pull. *"Boing!"* I say, causing a full-blown cackle and enthusiastic clap from Elodie.

"More," she says and signs at the same time, pushing both fists together. "More *boing!*"

I do it again to Bex's hair and then turn and do the same to Elodie's hair.

Bex finishes putting on El's socks and boots and then stands, watching us with her hand on her belly. "I swear if this baby doesn't have red hair, I'm sending you back."

"Me?!" I ask, incredulous. "You're the one with the stronger DNA!"

She steps in, wrapping her arms around my waist before laying her chin on my chest. "You know I only married you so we could have red-headed children." She raises an eyebrow and looks pointedly at Elodie, not a red hair in sight.

"Yes, darling. I'm so sorry to have failed you so egregiously. However can I make it up to you?" I tease.

"I'm sure I can think of a few ways." She kisses my nose and then turns toward Elodie. "Okay, my cabbage. Let's go ice skating!"

"Damn! Skate-ing!" Elodie says.

My arm shoots out, holding Bex back from pummeling Gabe. "I'll take care of it," I say. "You get loaded into the car."

"Fine. But make sure to rip him a new one!" She shakes her fist for emphasis. Indignant Bex is fucking adorable.

I salute her and then start looking for Gabe.

I find him poking at the presents that are already under the Christmas tree. "Gabriel," I chide, laughing as he nearly jumps out of his skin.

"Santa's Snowballs!" he exclaims.

"Much better. Stop teaching my daughter bad words," I say. "And if Bex asks, I really messed you up, okay?"

"Yeah, okay. Sorry about that. She's talking so much more than the last time I saw her," Gabe muses.

"She is half Bardot. You are a chatty bunch."

Gabe huffs. "Don't even think about blaming us—you're the one who never shuts up."

"Let's just say she comes by it honestly. You ready?"

He takes a deep breath, stretching side to side. "As I'll ever be."

Gabe seems a little solemn today so I ask, "Everything okay? Did you and Luci stay much later at Louie's last night?"

"I don't know man, I think—"

"Anders!" Bex calls from the front door. "Grab some snacks, please! I'm already hungry!"

I slap Gabe on the shoulder. "I want to hear about it later, yeah?"

"Yeah." He nods, sighing. "Yeah, let's talk later."

———

Bex has had a bag of goldfish, nachos, and hot chocolate from the concession stand, and half of my churro. I can see she's fading fast, and both my girls are going to need a nap soon.

I skate over to the edge of the rink where Bex is leaning up against the boards. Planting a kiss on her forehead, I ask, "You still grumpy, Baby Bardot?"

Her brows furrow. "I'm not grumpy," she protests. She's so cute when she's a little pissed. I take my glove off and push her pout up into a smile.

"You're pouting."

She pouts even more, which I didn't know was possible.

"I just want to be out there with you and El! This is the first winter she's been skating, and I can't even go with you guys," she moans.

I tuck a curl behind her ear. "It's for your safety, baby." I reach over and rub her belly. "For the safety of the baby, too. You're like bambi on skates."

"If you're trying to make me feel better, it's not working."

"Okay, grumpy. I'm going to do one more lap with our daughter—you stay here and try not to make it obvious that you're staring at my ass the whole time."

She puts her head in her hand and sighs. "It's a nice ass, though."

I can't argue with her, so instead I wink and skate over to Elaine and Hugo. They are bracketing Elodie, guiding her on her baby skates as she giggles up a storm. She's such a happy baby, and I love that she gets to be a big sister.

I also love that I get to be a dad. I was so fucking terrified at first—I didn't exactly have a great example to model my parenting after. Between the Bardots and friends that we've made in New York, Elodie is truly being raised by a village of people who love us.

Elodie looks up at me as I get closer. Her chubby cheeks are rosy, and her gummy smile melts my heart. "Dada! Damn, skateing!"

Elaine busts out laughing at my toddler even though she's been saying those same two words the entire time we've been at the ice rink. "Yes, darling. Skating! You're doing a great job." I reach out and take her little mitten hands in mine. "Want to skate with Daddy?" I ask.

She nods enthusiastically in response to my question, and we take a slow lap around the ice. My quads are burning from skating backwards while bending down to her level, but it's worth it to watch how much she loves being here.

"Wave to Mommy!" We skate past Bex who can't decide if she wants to be grumpy or sentimental. Elodie lets go of my hand to wave but quickly loses balance. I scoop her up right before she falls on the ice and skate to the edge of the rink. "Alright, that's enough of that. Should we get more food and then we can go home for a nap?"

"No nap!" Elodie says at the same time Bex says, "God, a nap sounds so nice."

I look at Elodie and shrug. "Mom's the boss."

She pats me on the head. "Okay, Dada."

Bex unties Elodie's skates as I take mine off, and we walk over to the concession stand.

"Welcome back," the woman manning the stand greets us.

"I'd like more nachos and a fresh hot chocolate... Let's do a pretzel, too." Bex turns to me. "Do you want anything?"

"Oh, none of that is for me?" I ask, smiling at my pregnant wife.

"I'm growing a baby, killer. That's all for me." She contemplates for a moment. "I might share some of my pretzel with El."

"I have another bottle in the bag for El," I reply.

"Well then, it's all for me." She grins. "Are you ordering?"

I get my own nachos and drink, even though I know Bex won't finish hers.

We find a picnic table with a view of the skating rink so we can watch the rest of the Bardot siblings make a fool of themselves as they race around the rink.

Bex pops a nacho in her mouth and chews—her thinking face tells me she's trying to figure out how to say what's on her mind.

"Spit it out, Baby Bardot."

She looks at me quizzically. "My nachos?" she asks, her mouth still full.

"No, whatever it is you're thinking about."

"How do you know I'm thinking about something?"

I circle my finger around her face. "Because I know you. And that face means you're thinking about something important."

Said face scrunches up and then she sticks her tongue out at me. "I have some ideas for that tongue," I whisper.

"Anders!" she laughs, and then finally says, "Okay, I was thinking about something… What if you're disappointed?"

I'm confused. "Disappointed?"

"By the gender of the baby."

I immediately get up and circle the table, pulling her in and tucking her head under my chin. "Oh, baby. How long have you been worried about this?"

"Since I found out." Her words are muffled in my chest. I rub my hand up and down her back and then pull her away so I can look her in the eyes.

"Baby Bardot." I take her face in my palms. "I could never be disappointed in something that you made."

"We made," she corrects.

"Even better." I kiss her nose. "I will love this baby no matter what, because they're a part of us." I nod toward Elodie. "They are a part of this crazy little family we are building."

"I just want them to have red hair," she cries.

"Of course, baby." I go back to soothing strokes up and down her back. I can see sleep heavy in her and Elodie's eyes.

Bex takes two more bites of her food, and then she's ready to go. I wave down Gabe and point to Bex's unfinished nachos before nodding to the car.

We make it back to the house, curling up for a family nap in Bex's childhood bedroom. I watch as my girls slowly drift off, mirror images of each other. My chest hurts as I'm overcome with gratitude. I rub at the ache, and then twine my fingers with my wife's, slowly falling into a restful sleep.

Gabe's Santa duties start tonight. Each member of the family gets to open one present on Christmas Eve. It's not really a surprise though, because they always open up matching pajamas to wear to bed that night.

This year it seems as though we all get flannel pajama pants with a dancing reindeer pattern and a red long sleeve T-shirt with our names across the back. I pretend to act surprised when Gabe drops my present in my lap last.

He shrugs. "You were the last to join the family."

"Technically, I think that was Elodie," Jules chimes in.

"Obviously, El was going to be the first to get her present!" Gabe looks affronted, as if we personally wounded him.

"I'm fine being last," I assure everyone. I tear the wrapping paper off my gift as everyone watches. The first item on top is a tiny red onesie that says "Baby Bardot" across the front. I glance at Bex—her eyes are already on mine, watching.

"You will always be my Baby Bardot, but I'm excited to add another one," I tell her.

She smiles and nods toward the rest of the package. "There's more."

Obviously, my matching pajamas are in there as well, so I don't know why everyone is watching me so intently. I pull out the pants and wrap them around my neck like a scarf which makes Elodie laugh.

Then I pull out the shirt, opening it to reveal my name across the back. But instead of my name, it says, "Girl Dad?" I ask.

I look around a little confused before landing on Bex. She has tears in her eyes, and she's biting her lip. She rubs her belly and repeats, "Girl Dad."

"It's—" *Holy shit.* "It's a girl?" I choke on the last word as a tear finally falls down Bex's cheek. She nods again and my eyes begin to sting.

"It's a girl!" Elaine screeches. "Oh, El, you get a baby sister!" She swoops down, picking up my daughter and hoisting her into the air. They do a celebratory dance around the living room, Elodie sitting happily on her LaLa's hip.

"Sit-ter," Elodie parrots, clapping and dancing even though she doesn't truly understand what's happening—she's simply matching the joy she sees on everyone's faces.

Jules hops up from his spot on the couch, calling over his shoulder, "This calls for celebratory sparkling cider."

Hugo pulls down the fancy champagne glasses, pouring a glass of sparkling cider for all of us. Elodie even raises her bottle as we *cheers* the newest member of the family. I tug Bex under the mistletoe that Elaine has hung up in the door frame and kiss her senseless, her family whooping and laughing the whole time.

She pulls away breathless. "You aren't disappointed? You wouldn't prefer a boy?"

"Are you kidding? I get another mini-you." I smile. "I couldn't be happier, Bex," I whisper, leaning down to nip at her earlobe. "I love you."

Her eyes are shining again when she says, "I love you too, killer."

Elodie has finally fallen asleep in her crib in the spare bedroom. She was wired, high on the excitement we all have about adding to the Bardot family. One of my favorite parts of being off work is singing lullabies to my daughter, so I didn't mind the extra snuggles.

And now, I get to show my wife just how excited I am about being a girl dad—again. I quietly shut the door to the room Bex and I are sharing, laughing when Bex opens one eye and says, "Took you long enough."

"El was extra snuggly tonight. I wasn't going to pass that up," I reply, sliding under the covers next to her.

"She's a daddy's girl, for sure." Bex smiles and my hand finds hers, tangling with it under the thick quilt she has pulled up to her chin.

Her grin turns from sweet to wicked as she guides my hand to her hip. Her *very naked* hip. "I have something else for you," she murmurs. Her eyes dart to my mouth as she licks her bottom lip.

"Rebecca," I warn, knowing my stern tone gets her off. "What will I find if I take this blanket off?"

She bites the same bottom lip she was just licking and looks up at me through her thick lashes. "Why don't you find out?" she challenges.

I hum, loving when she pushes my buttons just as much as she loves doing the pushing. My hand releases her hip and slowly tugs the quilt down. The first thing I see are Bex's perky pregnancy tits—*God, I love pregnancy tits*—wrapped in a red silk bra. An underwire half-cup situation helps push them up, and a large ribbon looking thing is tied in a perfect bow across her nipples.

"Fuck me, Baby Bardot," I groan.

"That's the plan," she brats, pushing up from where she was laying so she can prop one elbow on top of the pillows behind her. When she lays like this, the blanket slides down exposing part of her pregnant belly and places her nipples directly in line with my mouth. I can't help but lean forward and lick one through the fabric bow, which grants me a pleased sound from my wife.

I continue to lick and suck at the skin of her cleavage as I inch the covers down to expose more of her. I realize her hip wasn't naked like I originally thought, but instead, a thin strap wraps around it, leading to another bow right at the top of her ass.

"Where the fuck did you get this?" I ask, my eyes drinking in the sight of her laid out just for me.

She frowns slightly before answering. "I was feeling so frumpy last week when my stomach really started to pop. I feel so much bigger than I felt at this time with El." I reach out and soothe the furrow in her brow.

"You know I think you're beautiful," I mutter, kissing the tip of her nose.

I can feel her eyes roll. "I know, but I wanted to *feel* beautiful. So I went down to that lingerie shop down the street from that Thai place we like and spent probably way too much money." She shrugs. "It seemed like a good idea at the time."

"Oh, it was"—I lick a line down her jaw—"a very"—a suck under her ear—"good idea." I punctuate my thought with a tug of her ear between my teeth. "Get on your knees," I command, a soft whisper that makes her shiver.

"Yes, Daddy," she replies, instantly making my cock harder.

She gets on all fours, presenting her ass to me like the present it is. I push her wild curls over her shoulder and trail my finger down her spine, until I get to the bow. I'm about to tug on it when Bex's words stop me. "They're crotchless," she says, knowing eyes meeting mine over her shoulder.

Fuck, she's sexy like this. It feels like the only time she actually listens to me, and I love the control she's able to hand over. Only ever with me. Only ever with each other.

My finger continues its exploration, slipping between what I can now tell are two straps that open up for easy access to her delicious cunt. "How wet will you be if I slide my finger just a little... bit... further, baby?" I tease down as I ask, circling the pucker of her asshole.

She moans, arching her back and attempting to push back onto me. I tsk, lightly smacking her right ass cheek. "Patience, Baby Bardot. You know this," I scold.

"Anders," she begs. "Please, baby."

I lean over, covering her back with my front. I'm still fully clothed up against her mostly naked body, and I'm loving every minute of it. I bite her exposed neck, and she rocks back into me again, grinding into my lap as much as she's able to. "Tell me what you need," I demand.

"You," she replies. "Anything—everything." She shakes her head, frustrated at the lack of friction.

"What did I say about patience?" I ask. "You know I'll reward it. Be *patient*," I remind her.

She nods, dazed. My finger resumes its teasing, slipping through her slick folds and circling lazily at her entrance. "You are so good for me, baby. So wet and..." I thrust a finger into her, curling to hit the spot that makes her moan. "Tight," I finish.

I sit back on my heels and watch as she rides my finger. "More," she begs, dropping to her elbows. But I don't listen. Instead, I continue my steady pace, watching as she gets more and more worked up. More and more agitated. More and more turned on.

I know my wife. I know what she likes. She might beg for *more, faster, harder,* but she loves to be toyed with and teased. She wants me to wring every last drop of pleasure out of her and that takes time.

She knows this.

I know this.

So I don't give her more—yet—and instead, I continue pulsing in and out of her tight pussy, my other hand reaching up to lightly wrap around her neck. She fucking *leans* into my hand, applying more pressure to her throat, a quiet whimper slipping through. I add another finger to her cunt so I can stretch her for me and hold there for a moment.

I wait until she relaxes slightly and then smooth my left hand down her throat and over the top of her breast. She whines at the loss of contact around her neck, but I remind her, "We can only play so much, Baby Bardot." I rub my hand down over her stomach. "I have to protect what's mine," I growl.

She sighs in understanding before muttering, "Fatherhood is making you soft."

That earns her another slap to her ass. I push my fingers into her and then pull her up onto my lap so she can feel exactly how *soft* I am. "Soft, huh? How soft is my cock? I know you can feel exactly how 'soft' you make me," I mock.

I can't spank her again, so instead I reach down and pull the bow at the top of her ass, releasing swiftly, allowing it to snap back. I instantly feel her tighten around my fingers. "Fuck, you love that, don't you? That bratty mouth loves when I punish it." I think for half a second, making up my mind quickly. "On your knees. The floor this time."

Bex moves quickly to the edge of the bed, getting down on her knees. Her curly hair halos around her head making her look like some sort of Christmas goddess. It sounds ridiculous but the red silk bow across her tits is begging for me to yank the fabric, unwrapping the ultimate gift.

My finger runs along the edge of her jaw and tips her chin up to me. Her soft lips part, releasing a quiet pant. "Ready to put that bratty mouth to good use?" I ask.

Her eyes darken, meeting mine as she nods enthusiastically.

"Good girl." I unbutton my pants, standing. Her hands automatically come up to my waistband and she pulls down.

"You never wear any fucking underwear," she laughs, abruptly stopping when my cock springs free.

"If that was truly an issue for you, I'd start wearing underwear." She wraps her hand around my shaft and strokes until she gets to the bead of pre-cum at the tip. My next words are strained. "My guess, though, is that your perfect cunt is dripping from the sight of my cock in your hand. So I think…" I pretend to weigh my decision, and Bex responds by sticking her tongue out and licking my tip. "*Fuck.* Yeah, I think I'll keep making things easy for you to access."

She grins wickedly up at me, pulling my pants the rest of the way off, and then gets to work. Bex used to be unsure in her movements when sucking me off, but she's confident now. She wraps those plump lips around me, taking me deep into her mouth. Her hand wraps around the base, covering what her mouth can't quite reach. She pumps up and down, her tongue pressing up against the underside as she sucks.

We both release a loud moan, and then our eyes instantly widen in tandem as we remember where we are. Bex doesn't come off me but her eyes do crinkle at the corners in mirth.

"Something funny?" I grit out.

She does pop off then, a string of spit still connecting us together. She wipes her mouth and then says, "Did I ever tell you about the time Mom asked me if I knew how to pleasure you properly?"

"Fucking hell, Baby Bardot."

She laughs again and then her smile turns coy. "Well… do I?" she asks, looking up at me with swollen lips and watery eyes.

"Nothing," I start, cupping her cheek in my hand. "Nothing could ever bring me more pleasure than you do, Rebecca. You are the other half of my soul. My heart outside of my body. You, and you alone, bring me more pleasure than I have ever deserved."

She blinks, registering my words. "Good answer," she whispers. And suddenly, I don't want her on her knees anymore.

"Come here, baby. Let me make love to you." I stand her up, pulling her underwear off before I guide her back onto the bed. Leaning against the headboard, I settle her on my lap, loving the way she slides over my cock with her slick heat.

She reaches down to the hem of my shirt, and I lift my hands so she can remove it. Once I'm totally naked, I reach up and toy with the bow across her chest. "May I?" I ask, tugging lightly.

Bex nods once and I pull down, untying the bow and revealing her perfect breasts. She hisses as I suck one of her nipples into my mouth, my hand coming up to find the other. She reaches down between us and positions the head of my cock at her entrance. I let her slowly slide down, restraining myself even though I desperately want to piston up into her.

Once she's slid down to the hilt, she leans down so her forehead touches mine. Her eyes are screwed shut and she whispers, "Feels so good. So full."

"Take your time," I whisper, leaning in even more to take her lips with mine. We kiss lazily as she gets comfortable. She slowly starts to move up and down, her tongue getting more desperate and possessive against mine as she goes.

Eventually, she moves faster, her tits bouncing beautifully for me. I tweak her nipple and move my other hand between her legs to circle her clit. That sends her head falling back in pleasure, exposing the column of her throat to me.

Keeping both my hands where they are, I also lean in and suck *hard* where her shoulder and neck meet. That causes Bex's jaw to drop open, a whine slipping out. "I'm so close," she whispers. "So, *so* close."

I bite down and she explodes, waves of her orgasm crashing over her. "Look at me," I command, and her eyes pop open. Her mouth is still wide in pleasure, and the fucking picture she paints sends me over the edge too. My thrusts become erratic, but I try to keep my thumb on her clit as her thighs vice grip around mine.

We continue moving through the aftershocks until neither of us can take it anymore, and Bex collapses against me, my dick growing softer inside of her.

I rub slow circles up and down her back, massaging the knots that have formed in her shoulders. She groans, kissing my neck, and I shudder. We sit there like that, soaking each other in until she gathers enough strength to waddle to the bathroom.

"Your cum is dripping down my leg, killer."

I follow her into the bathroom, turning the shower on. "Sounds like we need to clean up," I say.

She yawns but nods, stripping her bra off. I come up behind her, kissing across her shoulder and rubbing her belly. "My wife," I murmur between kisses. "My baby." I circle her stomach again.

"I love you," she sighs, relaxing into me, a smile playing at the corners of her lips.

"I love you," I reply.

Contentment washes over me, as it often does when I pause to take stock of our life together.

It stays with me through our shower together. It stays as we dress in our matching family pajamas and crawl into bed together. It stays as we kiss some more, wishing each other a Merry Christmas between kisses. It stays and stays and stays.

Contentment stays, and I know it always will. And for that, I will always be grateful for Bex, and Gabe, and this family that so quickly accepted me as one of their own.

Eventually, we both fall asleep, sated and exhausted and so incredibly happy.

7
ELAINE BARDOT
December 25th

"I'm only a morning person on December 25th." — Unknown

"Merry Christmas, *mon chou*," Hugo whispers. I feel the bed dip, and my eyes crack open to see the very early dawn light streaming through the curtains.

I've never been one for early mornings, but, thankfully, I married a man who is the epitome of "morning person." He's sitting on the duvet next to me with a steaming mug of coffee, little Christmas trees hand painted around the perimeter. A soft smile graces his lips causing the wrinkles at the corner of his eyes to deepen.

"Merry Christmas, my favorite cabbage," I croak, my voice gravelly from sleep. "Is that for me?" I ask hopefully, eyeing the mug.

"Of course, but—" He pulls the mug away when I reach for it. "It's still too hot. You'll burn your tongue."

A small smile tugs at my lips, and I reach up, patting his cheek. "Always looking out for me," I sigh.

"Over thirty years we've been together, and yet you still drink the coffee too soon and burn your tongue. Every damn time," he mutters, leaning in to place a kiss on my forehead. He sets the mug just out of my reach, ignoring my protestations.

"Why did you even bring it up here if you weren't going to let me have it?" I raise an eyebrow at him in question.

"To get you out of bed," he declares. "Everyone is downstairs already, waiting for the sleeping beauty—our fearless Bardot matriarch."

That information perks me up. While I do love to sleep in, I don't want to keep everyone from the day's festivities. With everyone under one roof last night, I did sleep more peacefully than I have in quite a long time. I feel as though my heart is whole when we are all together.

I swing my legs over the side of the bed as Hugo stands, offering me his hand. He gives me another peck on the nose once I'm standing before him and then one on the lips because the man can't help himself. "You have five minutes," he whispers against my lips. "Don't touch the coffee yet. I'm heading downstairs—know that your eldest will riot if he can't start passing out presents soon."

"It's never taken much to make Gabriel riot," I challenge. Hugo's laugh rumbles in his chest, the sweet smile still gracing his lips.

He walks toward the door, turning before he leaves. "Yes, well, I've always said he's a lot like his mother in that sense." He leaves before the pillow I lob hits him. It *thwacks* against the closed door instead and lands in a heap on the floor.

Four minutes and thirty seconds later, I'm walking down the stairs as Gabriel is coming up.

"There you are!" He throws his hands into the air, looking much more like the little boy that used to fuss at his siblings than the thirty-two year old man he's supposed to be.

"Merry Christmas to you too, my cabbage." I get to the stair step right above him and smooth his hair back off his forehead. "Patience has never been your strong suit."

I bop him on his wrinkled nose and then take a sip of my coffee, now the perfect temperature.

He waves his hand in front of his face. "Don't bop me! It's been so long since I've been Santa! Let me have this!"

"Okay, darling," I soothe. "Let's get started, shall we?"

We continue down the stairs together until I see that everyone is lounging in the living room, not nearly as anxious to start our morning as I'd initially been led to believe. Everyone except Elodie, that is, who seems to be vibrating with excitement as her father tries to distract her from the giant pile of presents under the tree.

She spies me and her hands fly up above her head. "LaLa!" she screams, waddling toward me. "Peh-sants!"

"Yes, love. Lots of presents!" I reply as she barrels into my legs, wrapping her chubby arms around them. Her brown curls poke this way and that, hazel eyes shining up at me. "Do you want to open one?" I ask her. She runs and jumps back into Anders' lap, clapping wildly.

Gabe looks around the room. "Can I start now?" His excitement matches Elodie's, while everyone else seems just as tired as I am.

Ben smashes a couch cushion over his head, grumbling, "Why is everyone so loud?"

Jules is sitting next to him and replies, "It's not our fault you finished the whiskey by yourself last night."

Ben points his finger toward Gabe. "He helped. I don't understand how he's so cheery right now."

"Enough out of you," Gabe says, piling his arms with gifts to pass out. Elodie is first, of course, unwrapping a bag of goldfish crackers. We all laugh as she squeals in delight at the sight of her favorite snack.

Bex was explicitly clear that she did not want us to shower Elodie in gifts. First of all, because she is one and really has no need for a bunch of random things. And second of all, she said their New York apartment is entirely too small for lots of toddler items, especially with baby number two on the way. That meant that Jules and I spent much of last night wrapping up various snacks so El would have lots of presents to unwrap today.

We respect Bex and Anders' parenting choices. However, that respect didn't stop me from getting Elodie a doll house that will stay here for when she visits. And several dolls for her to play with. And a box of books. And some new puzzles. She is the first grandchild, after all.

We take turns opening the rest of the presents, Gabriel, unsurprisingly, making his brothers wait until the very end before he passes anything out to them. To his utter dismay, they don't much mind, all of us entranced by the littlest Bardot-Olsson.

I find my way next to Bex on the other couch, rubbing her back as she watches her daughter open snack after snack with childish joy. She leans her head on my shoulder and whispers, "I'm nervous."

Not an easy admission for her to make, I know. I move her head down to my lap so I can braid her hair as we talk. "What are you nervous about, *ma petite chou*?"

She sighs, rubbing her hand mindlessly up and down her stomach. "Two girls," she finally says. "I don't know what to do with sisters! I don't have any of those. What if I'm a bad girl mom?"

I tut, letting her words hang. She thinks a bit more. "I miss it here," she says moments later. "I didn't know that having kids would make me need my mom, but I do. I need all of you guys. It's lonely doing this in the city, just the three of us."

"Oh, darling. I can come down more often," I reply. "You've always been so independent. I never wanted to squash that in you."

"You haven't!" Her reply is quick and emphatic. "I... I don't know. You are a great mom and we"—she gestures around the room—"are all so lucky. It feels like a high bar that you've set."

Her sincerity makes my eyes sting. "I love all of you. Your

father and I have four amazing children. You and Anders have built a beautiful life and family together, as well. You, my cabbage, are an amazing mother. Don't try to be me—be *you*. That is exactly what Elodie and her sister will need."

Bex nods, turning her head to give me a small smile. "We are going to try to move back soon, I think. I always wanted to get away, and now I feel that same desperation to return," she laughs.

I shrug, continuing to twirl her curls around my finger. "Things change. People change. That's a good thing, Rebecca."

She tucks her hands under her chin and murmurs, "Thank you, Mom."

Hugo catches my eye from his spot across the room, a question on his face. *She's fine,* I mouth. He seems satisfied by that answer, standing when the oven timer dings.

"That'll be the breakfast casserole," he says to a room that is not really paying attention to him. I see Jules notice his dad walking into the kitchen. He gets up to follow, and I frown at his retreating form.

Bex and her family will be fine, I truly do believe that. The rest of these boys, however, are worrying me.

―――

Christmas day has been utterly perfect. We've eaten entirely too much, Elodie has played with all of the toys we were not supposed to get her, and the weather was nice enough to bundle up and take a quick walk around town.

Now, Hugo and I are snuggled together on the loveseat, everyone more or less in the same position they were when I came downstairs this morning except Elodie, who has already gone to sleep, and Bex, who doesn't look like she's far behind her.

I sip on another mug of spiked hot chocolate and consider my children. I heard whisperings today of Ben coming home, and Bex also seems ready to return. My hopes are up, whether I want them to be or not. Now I just need to figure out how to make sure they follow through.

"You have your scheming face on," Hugo whispers. "Should I be scared?"

I think about my answer before I reply. "I don't think so…"

Hugo hums, seemingly unconvinced. "Well, just don't make anyone too angry."

"Anger can be a good thing, darling. It fuels." I smirk. "But the boys need a shake-up, I think. They are all unhappy."

He frowns. "I don't know that you're wrong… what are you planning to do about it?"

"They need a little meddling. It will be good for them. Partners, job shifts, location shifts… something," I contemplate.

"Having those things won't necessarily make them happy. They need to do some inner work, first," Hugo adds.

"I agree." I watch all three of my boys—study them as they lounge and talk to each other, no one paying us much attention. They are so different from each other, but they all have their father's capacity for love. And my sense of humor, even when it's in a quiet way.

I tap my chin with my index finger. "Who should I start with? That's the real question," I whisper conspiratorially. My husband's huff makes me giggle, which draws the attention of our children.

"Oh no," Bex groans. "Whatever you two are planning, stop it right now!"

Hugo looks at her, his expression serious. "Whatever are you talking about, *mon chou*?" I see the dimple threatening to pop as he holds back his smile.

"The last time she meddled, I think it worked out pretty well," Anders chimes in, his eyebrows bouncing up and down.

"Leave me out of it," Jules says, staring straight at me.

And I think I found my target.

"Of course." I smile, rising from the couch. "Your father and I are going to bed. Merry Christmas, my cabbages."

I walk around the room and give each of them a kiss on the top of their head. Jules is last and when I get to him he murmurs, "I'm serious, Mom."

He's always serious. "I know, darling."

"Why doesn't that make me feel better?" he asks.

"It shouldn't." I grin. Then Hugo and I go upstairs and enjoy the rest of our evening—alone.

8
THEA ROSE
December 25th

"You have such a pretty face. You should be on a Christmas card." — Buddy the Elf, Elf

"It's too fucking cold here."

"Dad!" I chide. "Little ears!" I motion toward my four-year-old, Chloe, who is trying to press her nose against the truck window. We've had a long day. I scraped enough money together to buy her a few presents, and after playing with the used Barbies I found at the thrift store for most of the afternoon, I decided it was time to get out of the house.

We went to our favorite Chinese restaurant for a late lunch, then I convinced Dad to stop at a park, but we didn't last long before it got too cold, even with all of our layers. We piled in the car and started to drive around to look at Christmas lights. That was about an hour ago, and when I look back toward Chloe, my eyebrows furrow—I can tell she's getting sleepy, and it's probably time to head back home.

My dad grumbles at me, so I look back toward him. Christmas lights are flashing behind him as we drive through a well decorated Boston neighborhood. "She probably didn't even hear me," he mumbles.

"I did!" Chloe chirps from the backseat. "Mom says we shouldn't say fuck, even you, Pop."

I hold my hand out toward her as if to say, *See! She hears everything!*

Dad just laughs at her, a full belly chuckle. He and Chloe are the best of friends, especially with how much I have to work. The bar is closed for Christmas which is the only reason I'm able to drive around with them, and I hate to admit he was right, but it is particularly cold here.

We've been up north for almost ten years now, but Dad never misses an opportunity to talk about how much he misses Texas. We try to go visit a few times a year—what little family we have left is still there—but I don't miss it as much as he does, which is why we are living here in Boston. The summer heat alone is enough to make me avoid any state south of Virginia.

"You working tomorrow?" Dad asks, turning down another tree-lined street where all the houses have lights twinkling in the growing darkness.

"Yeah, night shift. I put it on the calendar," I remind him.

"I never look at that damn thing," he replies.

I sigh because I know he doesn't. "It would be helpful if you did look at it, Dad."

"You know I don't have anywhere else to be. You don't have to worry about Chloe either, you know that, too," he reminds me.

"Thanks, Dad," I mutter. I am grateful for him and his help with Chloe, I really am, but I also feel *so* incredibly lonely sometimes.

We stay quiet for the rest of the drive, the sound of Christmas music playing through the stereo and Chloe's constant chattering to herself. That girl loves to talk, and she does not care if anyone is listening. I try to listen, chiming in to answer a question every now and then, but as the questions grow further and further apart, I know Chloe is fighting sleep.

Dad knows it too because he starts to make his way back toward our apartment in Jamaica Plains.

When we get there, I scoop Chloe out of her carseat and carry her up the stairs to our apartment. Her head rests on my shoulder, her blonde hair fanning around her face. She's already in her pajamas, so I walk straight to the room we share and start to tuck her in.

"I love you, baby," I whisper as I kiss her forehead.

Her little hands are so sweet, still dimpled like when she was a baby. They come up to the sides of my face and pull me down so she can give me a kiss on my forehead too. "I love you, Mama," she says.

"You are my favorite Chloe," I say, something I tell her every night.

"You are my favorite Mommy," she replies before rolling over and cuddling with her stuffed bunny.

I smooth her hair back and kiss her again, before I stand up to leave. Her little voice stops me right when I reach the doorframe. "Next Christmas will be better, Mama."

I don't know why she says it. I mean it's not like today was great, but she's four so I don't know how she knows that. I stand there, stunned and immensely... sad. "Yeah, baby," is all I can say before I leave, shutting the door behind me.

Next Christmas will be better... I hope she's right.

MORE FROM RACHEL

Did you fall in love with the Bardot family?
Read Bex & Anders' story now!
Yours, Unexpectedly
And be on the lookout for book two in the Bardot Siblings series coming Spring 2025!

You can also join Rachel's Facebook group, Rachel's Romantics, for the latest updates, sneak peeks, and bookish fun!

Find signed books and merch at www.rachellewiswrites.com!

Xo, Rachel

ACKNOWLEDGMENTS

First and foremost, I want to say thank you to my readers! Your response to *Yours, Unexpectedly* inspired me to keep going. It has truly been the most fun diving back into the world of the Bardot family. They are wild, considerate, and so full of love. I hope they filled your cup the way they fill mine!

To all the book people I've met along the way: thank you for constantly encouraging me to keep going. Thank you Margarita Monday friends for keeping me entertained in the group chat and always being the ultimate hype girls! Thank you to Ray Riley who has become so dear to me, Peyton Corinne who is the reason this novella is not a prequel, and Jennifer Chipman who literally let me stay at her house when I visited! Thank you Joelle for always being willing to listen to my insane plot ideas, Sadie for making sure I know how to use commas, and Cathryn for the beautiful formatting! Thank you Brooke for helping me with graphics (including the cute family tree!), Kelsey for designing a gorgeous cover, Victoria for doing an amazing website overhaul, and Jess who makes the most beautifully aesthetic TikToks. Thank you to Neely, my favorite podcast co-host! Thank you to my alpha/beta readers: Jess, Kalie, Adrienne, Emma, Marina, Jennalee, and Kelsey. Thank you to my own real life book club who read *Yours, Unexpectedly* and hosted an author panel in Erin's living room! There are so many amazing book people in this world, I'm sure I'm forgetting someone!

To my friends and family: PLC – you are the ones who keep me sane and drive me insane all at the same time, but that's what framily is for! To my family (yes, all of you!), thank you for every kind and supportive word. Thank you for sharing my book in airports, with co-workers and book clubs, and with unsuspecting strangers. Thank you for taking the girls when I needed to get work done. Thank you, thank you, thank you!

To the Hugo to my Elaine, the Anders to my Bex: Bryan, I am grateful, always, for your unending support of this crazy dream. It is so special to have someone who looks at me when I say I want to quit my job, which would mean a major family transition, and says, "Let's do it." You are an amazing girl dad, partner, and friend. I love you!

Finally, to my girls. I hope that one day (a long time from now!) you come across my books, see this note, and know how much both of you inspire me. I wouldn't say I do it all for you, because I think it's important to show you that I did this for me, too, but I do a lot of this for you. So you can see your mom chasing her dreams, so you can know that it's never too late to try something you love, and so you never forget that girls run the world. I love you both!

ABOUT THE AUTHOR

Rachel Lewis is a fresh voice in contemporary romance with her debut novel "Yours, Unexpectedly". With charmingly flawed characters and laugh-out-loud dialogue, Lewis' writing effortlessly blends witty banter, delightfully indulgent spice, and heartwarming found families that readers will want to call their own.

Beyond her own writing, Rachel co-hosts the popular "Welcome to the Smut Show" podcast, where she engages with writers and bookstagrammers about their love of romance novels.

Rachel is a mother of two crazy girls, wife of a crazy husband, and crazy for some 90's country hits. She is a nostalgic TV watcher, lover of fan-fic, and is always willing to try a new color in her hair.

Find her on all social media platforms @rachel_mlewis or learn more about her and shop merch at rachellewiswrites.com.

Made in the USA
Columbia, SC
13 December 2024